TROUBLE ON THE OTHER SIDE

A Case of Unhappy Juice

DAWN WHEELER

Just A Thought Publishing
Michigan, USA

Also by Dawn Wheeler:

The Hypnosis I Know
The Secret Diary of Francis Lovell

TROUBLE ON THE OTHER SIDE
A Case of Unhappy Juice

Just A Thought Publishing
Michigan, USA

DEDICATION

I dedicate this book to the big blue marble-looking planet we call Earth and all the living beings who dwell here, in hopes that it will spark a revolution toward greater light, peace, unity, joy and goodness.

Please note, the bulk of this story was written during a time of great divisiveness and upheaval, not to mention a global pandemic. Life as we know it has seemingly been put on hold with no clear end in sight. I believe at this critical moment in time, humanity stands at a proverbial fork in the road whether it realizes it or not. These overwhelmingly uncertain and challenging circumstances are providing us with a rare opportunity to reset things and decide how all of us will go forward. Will we return to our old and ineffectual ways or will we boldly and bravely choose a different path? Will the paths that we take, lead to better lives and a better world? I hope so. Most importantly I hope people take a leap to find out.

ACKNOWLEDGMENTS

To my husband Philip - Thank you for your love, support, encouragement, humor and goodness. Thanks for also helping me come up with the idea for a story about a problem-solving department on the perceivably perfect Other Side and the fashion-conscious hottie that works there. You are a constant joy and inspiration. I love you.

To my departed mother Phyllis - Thank you for opening my eyes to the magic and mystery of the Universe and encouraging me to think outside the box. I love you and miss you.

To my proofreaders extraordinaire, Marie, Philip and Caroline - Thank you for your time, feedback and support.

ON THE JOB

The bright green message light blinks on and off in a steady rhythm. An important request awaits someone's attention. However, the occupants of this office have yet to begin their workday. So, the small round flashing button will have to wait.

Finally, the office suite's door edges open. Standing in the entranceway is an exquisitely beautiful woman with long, raven black hair, emerald green eyes, and rosy high cheekbones. Her thin curvaceous body is draped in luxurious purple silk and accessorized with the highest heels one could wear without toppling over.

"I'm back!" the enchanting female calls out to the empty office with a glorious grin on her face. "Aaah, another day," she says with a peaceful exhale as she heads for her desk, "another wonderful day!"

She means it too. Evangeline absolutely loves her job. She loves it so much she's been at it for more than one hundred and twenty-five years and is determined to do it many more years into the future.

Okay. I know what you're thinking. This is a fairy tale, the babblings of some crazy person or at least someone with a good imagination. I assure you Evangeline is completely real and everything you will read about her will be the absolute truth. How is this possible?

Well for starters, Evangeline does not live on the Earth, nor does she have a true physical form. She carries a physical representation, hence the curves and such, but she is really just a collection of energy and light that is encased in a projected facade. This outer illusionary shell enables her to not only appear as she would like, but it also simulates some of the senses she would have if it were real. For example, it lets her smell, taste and even change facial expressions based on how she feels.

While she may look the part and move and express in the same way human beings do on Earth, Evangeline doesn't have the constraints associated with a real physical body. There is no need for sustenance, sleep or going to the bathroom. More importantly, there is no pain. So where does this ball of energy and light spend her days? On the Other Side, of course. The Other Side? The Other Side of what?

On the surface, the world we live in could be viewed as a collection of physical objects like planets where physical structures and life forms may exist. Emphasis is on the physical. The truth is, despite having physical surroundings and bodies, living beings are not entirely physical. They're also comprised of mental, emotional, energetic, spiritual, personality and other intangible components. Moreover, everything on Earth including the planet itself vibrates at some frequency that's determined or influenced by these aspects.

The Universe that people think they know is actually made up of many planes of existence with often conflicting frequencies. All of them coexist simultaneously, yet their inhabitants may or may not interact with one another or even be aware of the other. Whatever their connection may be, together they form an ever-changing, multidimensional manifestation of reality. It is a reality that is more illusion than real, because it can change with the thoughts, beliefs, feelings, words and actions of those who live within it.

The Other Side refers to something that is beyond the Earth experience. It is a world that exists in the same place, but on a different frequency and at a higher vibrational level. At higher vibrations there is greater light and less density and darkness.

Unsurprisingly, these conditions also make it easier to create and sustain more positive circumstances. Thus, the Other Side offers its residents a far more comfortable, joyful and healing existence than what they may encounter on Earth.

Although visits to the Other Side are possible, dwelling there generally requires one to end their Earthly life and die. Once a person passes away, the essence of their being or soul continues on and can then transition to the Other Side.

Upon one's arrival there, physical constraints, illness and pain disappear. Health, comfort, strength, vitality and every capability and faculty they lacked or lost on Earth are restored. Aside from their bodies, those who cross over to the Other Side will likewise experience positive changes in their emotional state.

The Other Side does everything to promote a greater sense of calm and happiness within all who come there. Love, peace, beauty, comfort, ease and joy flow abundantly, while things like hatred and fear are a rarity and cannot be sustained. Vast amounts of information, resources and options are also made readily available to add to one's comfort, understanding, abilities and experience.

The Other Side is often described as being magical, wondrous, beautiful and infinite, along with many other favorable adjectives. Most notably, the Other Side is referred to as Heaven.

It is probably important to mention though, that the experience one may have on the Other Side can vary greatly by individual. The unique personality, beliefs, feelings, awareness and vibrational level of a soul will all have a significant influence on their transition to the Other Side. These aspects, along with the circumstances of their death, will also determine what they may see and do when they get there.

Unfortunately, these same factors could also cause a temporary obstruction to going to the Other Side in the first place. As a result, someone could become stuck in an in-between plane and have to wander around as a ghost until they can gain some awareness and resolution. The most common reasons for a soul to become a ghost are tragic or sudden death, lack of faith in something beyond death, fear, guilt, and confusion.

Even so, if a soul successfully crosses over to the Other Side, they may not be receptive to and thus experience all that it has to offer. At least not until they attain a higher level of awareness, healing and frequency that is.

Many often refer to the divider that exists between the Earth dimension and the heavenly Other Side as a veil. Just like the Other Side, the veil that separates it from the Earth is generally imperceptible to human beings. On the other hand, the Earth, along with many other dimensions or planes of reality is very much perceivable and accessible to the Other Side.

The Other Side is like command central to the Universe. This vastly complicated hub of activity and convergence of information is also essentially home base for every soul in existence.

While many select to occupy their time in other realms, everyone usually returns for some reason or another. How long they stay, will depend upon a wide variety of factors. Highest among them are perhaps a soul's growth objectives.

Given that learning and non-physical healing tends to be slower on the Other Side than in other dimensions like Earth, souls frequently opt to go elsewhere. Because of its near limitless opportunities for soul advancement, Earth is by far the most popular place for souls to spend their time.

When someone does come home to the Other Side, they will have seemingly endless options to choose from as to what they might do when they get there. Evangeline is one of those souls who prefer to stay on the Other Side. She has no desire to flit about the Universe or return to the Earth plane anytime soon. Yes, humans can incarnate onto the Earth many times, but we'll talk about that later.

Evangeline's last time on Earth was in the late 19th century. Tragically, her life was cut short by an infection she developed after sustaining what one would consider a minor injury. She died just days before she would reach her twentieth birthday.

Evangeline lived in what many called the "Deep South" of the United States of America. She grew up in the aftermath of a time of great divisiveness and war. Though sheltered for the most part, and never lacking any of the necessities of living, she suffered because the people around her had suffered. A darkness had overcome the world, and it would seem, there was a shortage of light to counteract it. Many people found it difficult to recapture some of the peace and joy they had before their worlds turned upside down.

Though her family was luckier than most, they were still people who endured. These men and women were not lighthearted or prone to frivolity. They were practical, hardworking people who learned to put one foot in front of the other, because the alternative was too difficult to consider. No one was coddled or indulged with reassuring words or affection.

Evangeline was taught early on that life was hard. As such, she would need to be tough and follow the rules that were set upon her or things would get even harder. It wasn't something she could forget even if she wanted to. The sour expression seemingly etched into her grandmother Cordelia's face and the constant negativity and warnings spewing out of the old woman's puckered lips were always there to remind her.

Because she did not think or feel the way others around her did, Evangeline felt as if her very spirit was under siege every day of her life. Looking back on that lifetime, she realized that despite having a lot of people around her, she felt very much alone. She also felt trapped with no perceivable way out.

Everything was decided for her from the moment she took her first breath. It started with her name, and then to what she wore or who she spent time with, and even what she would do on a daily basis.

Her parents called her Dorcas Bertha Beauregard. She was named after two aunts from her father's side, Dorcas Ethel and Bertha Gertrude, both of whom she hated with a passion. From their foul dispositions to the permanent scowls they wore on their weathered faces, these women were unpleasant in the best of times. And while their ugly names were perfectly suitable to who they were, they were an insult to everything that Evangeline was. She loathed her name so much; she absolutely refused to respond to it.

Her mother and father eventually grew weary of arguing with her and ended up just calling her "Daughter". Others who wanted to gain her attention would follow suit by referring to her by the type of relationship she shared with them, such as "Friend" or "Cousin".

As a result, upon her arrival at the Other Side she would choose a name for herself that was more to her liking. And if the moniker she used was more feminine or poetic sounding and perhaps symbolic of something positive or uplifting, even better. Of all the names she considered, Evangeline seemed to call to her the most. It made her feel oddly free and powerful.

Earthly literary buffs might recognize Evangeline as the name of a long and tragic poem by the famous nineteenth century poet Henry Wadsworth Longfellow. But this less than happy association would not deter her, especially because the word Evangeline also means "good news" in Greek. Evangeline likes to think that her soul's primary mission is to bring good news to those who need it most.

In her last physical form, she had dirt brown, extra curly, extra frizzy hair that required an excessive number of pins to keep under control. Of course, the heat and humidity of the South did not help. Now her hair is long, black, silky smooth with only the slightest of waves, and is always perfectly coiffed.

In her last life, she was more than plump and relatively shapeless. Her breasts, flat as pancakes, combined with her short stature and large frame, made it difficult to find something that fit her, let alone looked good on her. Not that her over practical and somewhat frugal mother would allow her much flexibility in her clothing choices, even if she wanted to see if she could look better.

But now Evangeline is slender and curvy in all the right places, tall, amply bosomed and she has all the clothes, shoes and accessories she wants at her disposal. She has actually become quite the fashionista and is always on top of the latest trends happening on Earth. She loves makeup, not that she needs it, since her skin is absolutely flawless. She adores wearing heels even though most people on the Other Side avoid them. Evangeline can't understand their hesitation, given that no one's feet or anything for that matter hurts on the Other Side. But souls are funny that way.

And while many inhabitants of the Other Side choose an appearance that is more of light and energy, Evangeline was very firm about taking on a physical representation. She admits the reason is in part because of all the constraints she had on Earth.

Having complete freedom on the Other Side provides her with infinite options to assert her true soul's essence and personality. Evangeline has no intention of wasting the opportunity or limiting herself simply because there is no need to define one's self with more physical attributes. Truth be told, she just finds it vastly amusing to do so.

While there are many others who choose to have a physical form like she does, quite a few of them gravitate to more simple dressings or adornments. Some take it to a level so bland and uninspiring however, she wonders why they bother. For instance, some souls prefer to move about in draped, shapeless robe-like coverings that make Evangeline want to gag if she could. Yes, they're comfortable to wear, but they lack the individuality and pizzazz that Evangeline embodies and desires. Thus, they will forever be banned from her energetic wardrobe.

Aside from her colorful personality and divine sense of style, Evangeline is also known for her tremendous attention to detail, superb problem-solving skills and ability to communicate with others. These qualities make her ideal for the job she has taken on during her time on the Other Side. To be clear however, souls do not need to have jobs on the Other Side. Having a job is just one of many ways one can occupy their time in this dimension.

Eager for some purpose or fulfilling activity, it didn't take long after Evangeline crossed over to the

Other Side before she decided that a job was in order. She originally learned about the position she now holds from her best friend, Annabelle, who she met shortly after arriving on the Other Side. Annabelle's longtime boyfriend, George, by the way, used to run the department Evangeline now works for, but has since moved on to something totally unrelated.

Annabelle works in the Jargon Slang Interpretation (JSI) department at Earth Works. Earth Works, commonly referred to as EW for short, is a huge complex that contains all the departments related to incarnations on Earth. Most Other Siders typically stretch out the pronunciation of the acronym to Ewwww to allude to the planet's less than praiseworthy features. I know, EW, that's pretty funny huh. Let's just say, a good sense of humor is essential when dealing with Earth stuff.

Unsurprisingly, souls have had a love-hate relationship with Earth since its creation. Everyone likes the idea of going there, well maybe not everybody, but most. On the other hand, once they get there, souls typically have a hard time recognizing and focusing on Earth's best and most desirable qualities.

Anyway, back to Annabelle. Her job at JSI is to document word meanings and usages on Earth over the years. Her efforts help ensure that researchers will always have proper context to interpret archival history. Annabelle's biggest pet peeve is for humans to use the same word to mean the complete opposite. Aside from the confusion it adds to the communication process, she thinks it's just plain stupid.

Case in point, the word "sick" has historically been used to describe someone or something that is ill or disgusting. While it continues to have the same meaning in current times, it now carries an additional connotation. "Sick" is now often used to characterize something as being really good or awesome in some way. This drives Annabelle absolutely crazy. But just like Evangeline, she can't imagine doing anything else.

As if keeping track of word meanings over time was not difficult enough, Other Siders muddy the waters by mixing jargon and slang from different periods on a daily basis. Many even enjoy using expressions from more recent Earth times despite their lack of exposure to them when they were living there. Aside from finding it amusing, they believe that by doing so, they will be better equipped to keep up with what people on Earth are doing.

Evangeline is one of those Other Siders who likes to intersperse current jargon into her daily speech, as do many of the souls she encounters in her job each day. She works just outside of EW in the Problem-Solving (PS) department in the Miscellaneous Stuff (MS) building in Head Quarters (HQ) center. Her department's primary role is to fix things that go awry on the Other Side.

One might probably think the Other Side is perfect and impervious to flaws or snafus, but because souls themselves are imperfect, even in the best of circumstances stuff can happen. You might say I get that, but…

With all the love and magic they have over there, couldn't they just snap their fingers or blink their eyes and make the problem go away with a poof? Given that souls can manifest pretty much anything on the Other Side just by thinking and intending it to be so; it would seem to be a logical assumption. After all, things like buildings, clothing, physical characteristics, scenery, music and food can be conjured up on a moment's notice. Problems, however, cannot be simply thought away.

It is an intentional design in the system, a purposeful flaw if you will, to keep souls on their toes and foster a sense of personal responsibility. Allowing souls to make mistakes or encounter issues and then resolve them, gives Other Side inhabitants the opportunity to grow and evolve even in the most positive circumstances.

Of course, the frequency of things going amiss is relatively small at such a high vibration. It thus makes it more feasible to have a single organization dedicated to solving problems for the entire Other Side. This prevents every department from having to keep someone on staff who just waits around until something goes wrong. It also allows their employees to be focused solely on fulfilling their daily requirements and responsibilities versus having to stop to address some concern. And let's face it; they may not have all that they need to resolve said concern, even if they had the time and opportunity.

Evangeline's "Fixers", as she likes to call them, have extensive knowledge and skills in a wide range of areas of expertise. Their experience, combined with the vast resources they have at their disposal, enables them to effectively solve even the most complex of issues.

Evangeline is responsible for initial information gathering, as well as making team assignments and coordinating their efforts. She also interacts with all relevant parties to obtain access or information for her team. In addition, Evangeline provides regular progress updates to both her own department heads and the heads of departments who are using their services.

Issues addressed by her team can be minor as well as major in impact and simple or complex to solve. They can span multiple souls and/or areas or be confined to a single soul and/or area. Each issue addressed by the PS department is assigned a level of urgency and seriousness from 1 to 5. The higher the number, the more critical the issue. Level 5s are exceptionally rare but do occur.

PS urgency levels are essential to helping the team in prioritizing their efforts, especially when there are more snafus to solve than usual. At the present time, the department has three outstanding cases, one level 3 and two level 2s. Her co-workers are hoping that once they are finally closed, something meatier and more exciting will come along. Evangeline can't help but think, *be careful what you wish for.*

After settling down at her desk, Evangeline quickly notices the blinking light beckoning her to listen to its message. She presses a silver button on the side of the device to stop the flashing and play the recording.

"Uh, Evangeline, this is um, Awesome-Curly, yeah yeah, I'll tell her, and um MacGregor is here too from Contracts," the voice on the message announces shakily. "We have a level 5. I repeat, a level 5. She knows how to get a hold of us, just be quiet. Yeah, sorry about that. Anyway, um, it's a level 5, so please get back to us as soon as you can. No, I am not going to ask her to bring us something to eat. Sheesh, you just ate a dozen donuts and two hot fudge Sundays. What? You need some protein? Where do you think you are? Oh, for goodness sake, you need to stop binge watching cooking shows on the Earth Channel. Get a grip dude! Now look what you made me do. You got me so distracted, I forgot to hang up. Sorry Evangeline. Thanks. Um. Talk to you soon. Um bye."

Evangeline lets out a long sigh and then mutters a simple "oh dear" before calling everyone in for an emergency meeting.

HOUSTON, WE HAVE A PROBLEM!

After apprising her team of their new problem request and its high level of severity, Evangeline heads over to the EW to meet with her new clients at Contracts.

The Contracts department is primarily responsible for negotiating the terms of incarnations on Earth. When someone decides to return there, they are required to establish a plan for their soon-to-be-new lifetime. A soul will sit down with their Guides and Guardians to work out the details of what they want to know, experience and accomplish during their time on Earth. They will ultimately subject themselves to challenging situations they hope to overcome and learn from. After all, time spent there is intended to be above all things, a learning experience.

Souls have ventured to this planet to hone and evolve themselves for eons. They knowingly sign on to play a game, which is essentially rigged against them, and try to win it as best as they can. Even though they will have no memory of what they agreed to and the odds are not particularly in their favor, they keep coming back for more.

Despite some pre-orchestrations, everyone gets free will, making this a very interesting game where no one really knows what will happen until the end. Souls engage in this uncertain and often highly uncomfortable endeavor, all in an effort to gain understanding, healing, knowledge or wisdom, and make their souls better.

Sadly, human beings have generally learned through suffering versus joy or some gentler means. Let's face it; people don't typically look for ways to improve their life when things go well. But when there's pain or adversity, they eagerly seek out answers and become more receptive to change. That which is negative has been the biggest motivating force for human beings since they came into existence.

Pain, illness, poverty, ignorance, fear, hatred, betrayal, jealousy, greed, judgment, selfishness, anger, oppression, prejudice, abuse, war and other negative aspects abundant on Earth have proven to be excellent catalysts for change. Through hardship, souls can develop kindness, compassion, generosity, love, unity, peace, acceptance of one's self and others, courage, strength, balance, ingenuity, wisdom and healing.

Tragically, and all too often, someone may not learn anything at all and continue to make bad choices and repeat undesired patterns over and over. Hence, most souls will have to utilize multiple lifetimes to get it right.

Souls may volunteer to serve as Guides and Guardians to help those whom they care about fulfill the objectives of their Earthly incarnations. Guides and Guardians play a vital role in providing hints, signs, intuitive nudges and impulses to help their charges remember who they are, and why they are there. They can also be of comfort and protection, and even arrange synchronicities to give clues as to the paths one should take. But Guides and Guardians are not permitted to interfere.

They cannot force anyone to take a specific path or prevent them from taking some path, nor can they violate a person's free will. Unfortunately, all too often, they will have to sit back and watch as the souls they care about struggle. Other than sending them love and signs of hope, there is little they can do about it. Yet, however difficult it may be to endure suffering or witness it, time and again, souls brave the harshness of Earth in hopes of improving upon themselves and the world. Is this noble or foolish? You decide.

Life purpose, lessons, challenges, along with the key players that will help them, are all decided upon before someone journeys back to the Earth plane. Key players? Are we talking about family members? Yes, we are. Therefore, if someone doesn't like their parents, they have no one to blame but themselves because they picked them. One's mother and father, along with everyone else who is critical to their life objectives are all prearranged before they step back onto Earth.

Souls also pick the environment into which they are born, be it poverty or wealth, freedom or oppression, peace or war or anything else that could help them fulfill their purpose. Even someone's gender is part of the grand plan to assist them along their path of learning and healing.

It's probably important to mention, however, that the circumstances one chooses may not be specifically tied to their own personal learning and goals. But rather, they could be intended to promote greater understanding and compassion, as well as healing for someone else and even the world.

Understandably, the task ahead can often seem overwhelming and potentially make someone feel reluctant to embark upon such a quest. As such, a beverage called "Happy Juice" is always administered prior to negotiations to help souls see and focus on the positive even in the worst of cases. This may seem subversive, but it's not. Every soul willingly drinks Happy Juice, because they know the potential for their soul to grow and heal is worth any pain they might experience to achieve it.

Happy Juice evokes a temporary state of pure bliss. The all-encompassing feeling it creates gives souls the courage, strength and perspective to do what will ultimately benefit them, even if they will moan about it later. Think of the extreme giddiness, comfort and calm you might experience after consuming the most potent of alcohol or drugs. Now multiply that by a trillion, and you will have some idea of what Happy Juice is like. It's O-Mazing!

Under the influence of Happy Juice, souls often agree to an excessively long list of incredibly difficult circumstances and goals without even a blink. They feel so good about what they are about to embark on, they often consider last minute additions. This is because they have no doubt in their ability to accomplish more if they tried. It's kind of crazy.

Under normal circumstances, no one in their right mind would accept even one quarter of what these souls have signed up for. Yet with Happy Juice it all seems easy peazy.

Of course, once someone gets to Earth, there isn't any Happy Juice to help them get through all the drama they requested to experience. The old expression, what doesn't kill you makes you stronger, certainly applies. And lest we forget, everyone on the Earth has free will, which makes the human experience even more complicated and uncertain. It's like walking into a different room every day, never knowing whether someone is going to hug you or kill you. Truthfully, it doesn't make a great selling point to go there. But it hasn't stopped billions of souls from doing it for eons. At least, not yet.

Well, there is a bit of an exception to this. Prior to being born, while floating around in the womb of their mother, a soul is given at least two undistorted and realistic views of what they signed up for.

One glimpse occurs within the first month or two, and the last one is provided just prior to labor and delivery. Another may be given somewhere around the half-way point if the soul requests it. At these moments, a soul can choose to stay the course or opt out. In more simple terms, they can decide to be born and go on living or they can miscarry or die.

It may be difficult to accept that souls can change their mind. Even the circumstances they were coming into can change. For these very reasons, someone may reconsider going forward with their plans. And while they can certainly modify what they've agreed to, some souls may choose to end their commitment to an Earthly incarnation anyway. Of course, there is also a potential for a soul to end their life early on because their parents agreed to experience a loss for their own learning purposes.

Sadly, the human beings who waited for a child and dreamed of a future with them are often left heartbroken and confused. More often than not, they may also feel like they've done something wrong and are being punished. But this is not the case. It's hard for the living to understand the spiritual aspects involved in what they experience. And again, without Happy Juice, suffering seems inevitable.

Evangeline takes the elevator up to the 10th floor. A melodic clang sounds as it reaches her requested destination. The huge golden doors part to let Evangeline exit. Her heels click against the shiny marble floors that line the hallway as she makes her way to suite 1000.

Just before she reaches the Contract department, she passes a door labeled "Container Assignment". She smiles as she remembers it wasn't that long ago when it was called "Body Snatching". But after the similarly named Earthly horror movie came out, the powers that be thought it prudent to change the name to something less fear invoking.

This department is one of the last stops a soul makes before returning to Earth. It is where they select the physical representation that they will be using on the planet for that time. Given that it was not at all to her liking, Evangeline suspects she ingested far too much Happy Juice before picking her last corporeal look on Earth.

Arriving at suite 1000, Evangeline nudges the glass door open and passes through a large waiting area. Multiple rows of comfy, teal blue chairs line the perimeter of the room. Small glass side tables, stacked with magazines from Earth, are positioned between every grouping of five seats. Evangeline makes a mental note to check before she leaves to see if they have a more recent copy of one of her favorite fashion magazines.

She walks up to the reception desk, a long steel and glass counter, where two males and two females are waiting to greet those who come there. All of them are dressed in those white robe-like things Evangeline dislikes, but to her amusement each wears their own unique set of accessories to jazz things up. For instance, one of the males is donning a baseball cap, sunglasses, and a coach's whistle which hangs down in front of him, ready to be blown.

The other guy has a cowboy hat on his head, a bandana tied around his neck, and a leather looking belt with a large silver buckle strapped around his waist. Evangeline wonders with a smile where his six-gun and holster were, and if he wore spurs under his robe.

As for the women, one of them has big, gold hoop-like earrings dangling from her ears and one too many, clinking, bangle braces adorning both wrists. Her long blond hair is swept up into a ponytail and secured by one of the biggest and sparkliest red bows Evangeline has ever seen.

The other female has punked out, purple hair with matching purple lipstick and eyeshadow, and dark lined eyes to complete the look. She also wears a spikey silver and black necklace and matching bracelet, 'cause every girl likes jewelry.

The cowboy speaks first. "Howdy," he says tipping his hat, "welcome to Contracts, where we are itchin' to make you a deal you can't refuse. How can I help you?"

Evangeline smiles as she thinks about how this guy is really pouring it on thick. "If you please," she practically drawls in her old southern accent from Earth, "I would be ever so grateful if you would tell me where I can find Awesome-Curly and MacGregor. We have a meeting scheduled that I am right near burstin' to attend."

"Well sure ma'am, all you need to do is make a left, just over there," he proclaims as he points. "Head down that hallway and then take another left. You'll be wantin' the second door on your right."

"Thank you most kindly, sir," she says with a slight curtsy. "One more thing, I am expecting a colleague to meet me here. Do you know if anyone has showed up yet?"

"Why yes ma'am. He arrived just a few minutes before you did." The cowboy gleams with pride at being able to provide such timely and important information.

"Oh, that's great. Thanks. Have a good day, you hear!" Evangeline practically skips away as she heads for the hallway.

The co-worker she is referring to is one of her top investigators. Given that this is a level 5, she thought it would be prudent to have someone with his skillset along for the initial meeting. He answers to the name of August, and sometimes Augustus when he's feeling a bit full of himself. August joined her team in 1985 and has been a valuable asset ever since. Intriguingly, prior to making his latest move to the Other Side, one could say his last three lifetimes were excellent preparation for the work he does now.

In the first of which, he was a reporter for a major New York newspaper until the stock market crashed in 1929. He was killed in a freak accident when a suicidal man leaped to his death and smashed into August before hitting the ground. August went back to Earth almost immediately.

This time he decided to become an operative for British intelligence. Unfortunately, his career only lasted one year and came to a sudden and dramatic end in 1956. Sadly, both he and the Soviet agent he was spying on and eventually convinced to defect were shot and killed before they were able to get to a safehouse.

August once again took the fast track back to Earth and spent his last incarnation in sunny and forever hot, Miami Florida working as a vice cop and detective. And no, if you are wondering, he never wore a white jacket or pastel shirt like Don Johnson did on the TV show Miami Vice. August would never be caught dead in anything so, so, he just doesn't have a word for it. Well maybe one word, yuk!

Clothing aside, the kind of work August did was serious business. Most of his cases involved illegal arms and/or narcotics. In fact, he died exactly one week after helping make one of the biggest cocaine busts ever, while simultaneously bringing down a drug ring in the process.

Shortly after attending a ceremony where he received a commendation for his efforts, August went out to celebrate at a local restaurant. Unknown to him or anyone at their table, one of his dishes contained an ingredient that he was highly allergic to. Unfortunately, it didn't take more than a bite before his throat closed up, his heart stopped beating and he was dead.

When August got to the Other Side he was understandably pissed. Obviously, he thinks the Other Side is pretty spectacular, but he couldn't help but feel cheated being cut down so early in his prime once again. But instead of jumping right back to Earth like he did in his last two incarnations, he decided to stay for a while.

He knew he needed to distract himself and take some time to get over the shock and anger of his most recent untimely demise. He therefore thought it prudent to put his energy toward something productive. August was not going to just sit around and relax with too much time on his hands to think about what could have been. Thankfully, PS seemed to fit the bill perfectly. And while he wasn't ridding the place of criminals, he was helping, nonetheless. This seemed to suit him just fine.

Unlike Evangeline, however, August saw no need to conjure up some physical representation for himself and feels perfectly comfortable flitting about as a ball of light and energy. He also likes not having to talk all the time. If he wants someone to know something, all he needs to do is direct his thoughts out to them. No muss. No fuss. Telepathic communication is the bomb! Well most of the time at least. If August is remiss and forgets to shut off his thought filter, everyone will know what he thinks whether he wants them to or not.

As a side note, the expression "the bomb" is just the sort of thing that Annabelle hates about the English language and its troublemaking brother slang. Let there be no doubt, if August actually had a head, it would be hit every time he used the reference in her presence. After all, bombs typically represent one of the most destructive forces on Earth. But as in August's context, they can simultaneously be used to mean something that's absolutely wonderful. This drives Annabelle crazy.

While August is a supreme professional on most days, he can come off a bit rough around the edges sometimes and has what many would call a crude sense of humor. For example, he finds it hysterically funny to let off noisy, smelly farts and burps, and blame others in his vicinity for carrying out the offenses. No one is typically spared the potential unpleasantry, except for Evangeline, that is. At least so far.

Evangeline knocks on a door labeled with a large green number four in its center. From behind it, she hears someone call out, "Come in."

She turns the knob and steps inside what looks like an Earthly conference room. In its center is a long, beige, Formica-looking table surrounded by plenty of cushy, rolling chairs that are covered in simple black fabric. Three of the walls are lined with tall, dark wood shelving that are nearly brimming with Earth artifacts and pictures. On the fourth wall, there's a large board and a projection screen that lowers down from the ceiling when needed.

Just to the right of the board, sits a rather sizeable food and beverage station. In its corner, there's a shiny silver tap coming out of what looks like an Earthly beer keg. But instead of it being labeled with some brewing company's brand name and logo, the area above the spout is adorned with a large yellow "H" and smiley face. Six glass beer mugs are lined up in two straight rows just below the tap, seemingly waiting patiently for the party to begin.

As you can safely assume, the content of the keg is Happy Juice. The euphoria-inducing beverage is dispensed this way, in hopes it will further add to a soul's comfort in transitioning back to Earth.

Seated around the table are two of the most magnificent examples of the human male species

Evangeline has ever laid her eyes on, along with her glowing associate August.

"Eh, they're alright" August says in her head, at which she tells him to get out of immediately before having her face flush red with embarrassment. Despite not having a real human body, physical representations on the Other Side include many details that add to the realism of the experience. Blushing is definitely one of those features she would gladly give up.

The two gentlemen Guides arise from their seats to shake her hand. Each of them is dressed in a brightly colored Hawaiian shirt with matching flip-flops and color coordinated shorts. They also have aviator type sunglasses perched on top of their heads just in case things get too bright, she supposes. All they seem to be missing are leis around their necks and perhaps a ukulele or some tropical drinks with umbrellas. Evangeline can't help but smile.

"I'm MacGregor, nice to meet you Evangeline," the stunning auburn-haired man with the most amazing green eyes says in a gentle Scottish brogue.

"And I'm Awesome-Curly," the dark-haired, Adonis with steel blue gray eyes proclaims. "But you can call me Awe. We really appreciate you coming here so quickly."

August starts to make gagging sounds in Evangeline's head and says "I can't help it if I'm awesome and I inspire awe. Oh brother. If only I had eyes, I would so roll them."

"August!" she blurts out in a warning tone, at which MacGregor and Awe's face register complete confusion. "Sorry" she says, leaving them even more confused. Thankfully, no one says anything.

As you may suspect, "Awesome-Curly" and "Awe" are made up names. For many years, Awe preferred to go by a name he had in a past life in Ancient Persia. Unfortunately, it was too difficult for his fellow Other Siders to pronounce, so naturally they felt a simpler nickname was in order. Because of his initial propensity to wear his hair long and curly and sometimes don a curly beard, everyone decided to call him Curly.

After many years went by, as buddies often do, Curly's friends would playfully tease one another. One day, after they were giving him a particularly hard time, Curly blurted out, "I'm Awesome!" in response. Being snarky as they were, his buddies decided to henceforth refer to him as "Awesome" when they called for him or told someone who he is.

To avoid confusion and help others transition to the new name, friends would frequently combine "Awesome" with "Curly". It didn't take long before the moniker stuck. Eventually however, Awesome-Curly decided to shorten the label to just "Awe".

"Alright, let's begin," Evangeline announces while turning on her recording device. "Please tell us what happened? What do you think is wrong?"

Awe declares without any hesitation that they have a serious Happy Juice problem. He looks down at his notes and then goes on to explain as best as he can what he believes has led them to such a disconcerting conclusion.

"A couple of days ago," he begins.

This is probably a good point to mention that the Other Side's concept of time differs greatly from that of Earth's. In reality, time is neither linear nor finite, regardless of how it is perceived on Earth. It is a never-ending dynamic which is essentially irrelevant on the Other Side. Despite that, residents of the Other Side often choose to reference it in the same way that Earth does. They find that doing so, helps them better relate to the restrictive measurement of time as it is experienced by those who dwell on the Earth.

Awe proceeds with his explanation. "MacGregor and I were sitting down to a normal Contract negotiation with someone who wanted to go back to Earthly England. When he first stepped in the door, he seemed happy and enthusiastic. He even brought some notes with him that he wanted to include in the Contract we would be drafting together. Then after some initial chit chatting, just like normal, we poured a glass of Happy Juice and had him drink it before the official negotiations could begin."

Awe continues with a long exhale of frustration, "I don't think even a minute went by before our guy started balling his eyes out. I couldn't imagine why he was so upset and asked him if he was alright. Ted, that's his name, then cried even louder and said he was just so sad, he couldn't bear it. MacGregor asked him what he was so sad about, and all he could say was that he didn't know."

"I stared at his empty glass mind boggled. I couldn't for the life of me understand why the Happy Juice didn't kick in, let alone why Ted came in the door pretty solid but was suddenly a wreck. I mean, we didn't even get to the first lesson on the list."

MacGregor nods and fidgets nervously. "Yeah, it was super confusing, and I felt really bad for the guy. I tried to say reassuring stuff and even offered to give him a hug. At that point, Ted broke into louder sobs and threw himself into my arms and buried his head in my chest. It was heart wrenching. I didn't know what to do and just looked at Awe, hoping something would come to us or that Ted would suddenly be ok again. But nothing changed. He was inconsolable."

"As I continued to hold him and try to calm him down, Awe ran out of the room to see if he could get some help."

"While Awe was gone, Ted told me there was no way he was ever going back to that 'horrible Earth' again. I was so confused, but I didn't want to argue with him, so I said he didn't have to go, which of course is totally true. I hoped it would make him feel relieved, but it didn't. In fact, he started to moan and shriek over and over about how terrible the Earth was. How much suffering it had. How much unfairness and unkindness there was. And then he proclaimed that no one should ever go there. Once again, I said he didn't have to go there. I then added that no one has to go there. They choose it. Unfortunately, this made him cry even more."

"Meanwhile," Awe chimes in, "I tracked down one of the counselors we have on staff to see if she had any ideas about what we can do. She followed me into the room and was shocked at what she saw and heard."

"'This is not normal,' she whispered to me. 'I know,' I said. 'So, what do we do?' The only thing she could think of was to give Ted an injection of a calming potion she had in her office. Thankfully, it did the trick and he started to become more rational and less emotional as time passed. But Ted still doesn't want to go back to Earth, and while he's not crying continuously anymore, he's not happy."

"Awe and I have known this soul for eons," MacGregor adds. "I've had four lifetimes with him, and Awe has been with him in three. Both of us have served as his Guide on a number of occasions. Ted's response is totally uncharacteristic of the soul we know him to be. While some degree of emotional response is expected when someone is planning a return to Earth, neither one of us have ever witnessed anything like this before."

"So, let me get this straight," August interrupts, "You have one guy who has a meltdown about going back to Earth and you think that means the supply of Happy Juice is compromised in some way?"

MacGregor clears his not-truly-physical throat and mentally counts to ten. He then tries to make himself speak as calmly as possible. "Respectfully, August, IT IS COMPROMISED! How much of it, I cannot say. But however reluctant you or any of us might be to admit that something is wrong, reality is reality."

He breathes out a long breath of frustration before continuing. "And oh, by the way, we don't have just one soul with an extreme and unexpected response. We have ten different unexplainable cases that would scare the bejeezus out of anyone. And every one of them occurred shortly after they drank Happy Juice. So yeah, to use the old Earthly expression from NASA's space program, Houston, we have a problem!"

OH DEAR!

"Alright everyone, let's just calm down for a moment," Evangeline urges. "There is no need for anyone to get their knickers in a twist. Let's be civilized and try to handle this like the reasonable and intelligent souls we are. And August…"

"No need Evangeline. I'm sorry guys. Really, I am. So, tell us about some of the other cases. Please."

Awe lets out a breath he didn't realize he was holding, before speaking. "Yeah, ok. Before I talk about the others, you should probably know that every soul who had an unexpected response didn't act the same way. Not everyone cried like Ted."

"So, what did they do?" Evangeline asks, feeling genuinely curious.

"Essentially everyone exhibited an exaggerated negative emotional outburst. Sometimes their response was specific to one feeling, like fear or anger, or in Ted's case, sadness. Then in a few cases, the soul would express multiple extreme feelings simultaneously," explains MacGregor. "And pretty much everyone made it absolutely clear that they had no intention of ever going back to Earth again."

"Thankfully, there is a positive to all of this," Awe proclaims with a crooked smile.

Evangeline looks at him like he is crazy or something. "Like what?"

"I don't know how familiar you are with the work we do here, but…" Awe begins to explain. "We generally conduct at least a few hundred Contract meetings every day. However, on the day when everything went wrong, we had less than twenty scheduled. If we were at our normal volume, it could have been a lot worse. Many more souls could have been affected."

"Wait a minute," August interjects, "why was your volume so low? Where was everybody?"

MacGregor decides to answer. "Most of the Guides were out of office attending a big convention near some mountain or volcano, so most Contracts were pushed out to a later date."

"Why didn't you guys go too?" asks Evangeline.

Awe chimes in. "Well, the reason why MacGregor didn't attend was because someone from his long ago, enemy's clan, the Campbells is the keynote speaker. Being that I am one of MacGregor's oldest and closest friends, I chose to stand with my buddy and stay away." Awe pats MacGregor's shoulder to emphasize the point.

"Thanks buddy," MacGregor says smiling. "Stinkin' Campbells! Of course, there was also the issue of them excluding food from the event," he adds with a frown.

"Yeah," Awe says with a look of sheer horror on his face, "can you believe it?"

"Um, I hate to point this out guys, but you don't need to eat food on the Other Side," August says with some hesitation.

MacGregor nods. "We know. But we like to eat. And there is no rule saying we can't eat if we want to. Anyway, who puts on a social function and doesn't serve food. It's totally uncool. I might even go so far as to say, it's barbaric."

Deciding to move the conversation along to something more relevant, Evangeline asks, "What about the other Guides? Why didn't they go?"

Awe shrugs his shoulder. "I suppose the others didn't attend because of the location or maybe just disinterest in the topics being discussed."

MacGregor suddenly jumps in, "or it could be the Guides against Guiding speaker."

August can't resist. He had to know. "Guides against Guiding? What are you talking about?"

"There is a small movement headed by this Guide name Larry O," Awe explains, "he wants to put an end to Guides guiding and only have them watch."

August laughs out loud. "That is the stupidest thing I have ever heard. If you don't guide, you are not a Guide. If you just watch, you are just watching. Unless someone is a sadist or sadomasochist, why would anyone want to just sit back and watch people make bad choices and suffer all the time and never try to help them do or feel something better? That is illogical and disgusting!"

Awe smiles and raises his hands in the air. "You are preaching to the choir August. Larry O is a nut ball, pure and simple. Nevertheless, the crazy dude has been getting some attention lately, so the convention organizers decided to let him speak. I can't imagine more than a handful of Guides sitting around listening to the guy. Regardless, some Guides are really mad that he's even being given any opportunity to spew his ridiculous ideas at all."

Evangeline points her finger to where August is hovering. "August, make a note to ask the other Guides why they stayed. Now let's table this whole issue and get back to some more examples of the extreme responses you talked about."

MacGregor hesitantly begins. "Alright Evangeline. Drake and Joanne were working on a Contract with a female called Vanessa. Just like Ted, they said she walked in the room with a positive attitude about being there. They even went so far as to describe her as being very chipper. Not too long after drinking her Happy Juice though, she appeared to be getting somewhat agitated. Because they were talking about her parent choices at the time, they didn't feel overly concerned."

"But then suddenly," he says with a pause, "she got really angry. They said that things got scary quick. Before they knew it, her anger rapidly escalated to rage, and she was breaking everything she could get her hands on. Vanessa shouted as she created destruction all around her. She even tried to punch Joanne."

MacGregor checks his notes again to make sure he says the next part right. "She started screaming about how there was a conspiracy and said that Drake and Joanne had a lot of nerve trying to send her to a planet where the game is rigged. 'How dare you ask me to pretend this is a good thing when it's pure torture,' she yelled. Then she rattled off a stream of colorful Earthly expletives and finally declared that she was not going back, and they couldn't make her. Vanessa then threatened to do harm to things outside the room if anyone ever asks her to go to Earth again."

"After receiving a calming potion injection, she stopped fighting and eventually crumpled to the floor. While no one has witnessed any further dramatic outbursts from her, she is committed to never going to Earth again. And just like Ted, Vanessa isn't particularly happy. She also has no desire to connect to anyone."

"Oh dear," is all Evangeline can manage.

"I second that," August proclaims in a shaky voice.

"Then there was James," Awe says with a weird look on his face. "Jabo and Fiona were assigned to his Contract. After the Happy Juice was administered, Jabo noticed James' eyes were suddenly filled with terror. Naturally, he asked James if he was ok. James whispered 'no' and then proceeded to crawl under the table and shake like someone who was trapped in an Earthly freezer. They tried to get him to come out from under the table, but he wouldn't budge. He started to whimper and tell them he wasn't safe."

"'They are out to get me,' he said simply. When Fiona asked him who he was talking about, he just repeated himself by saying 'they'."

"Of course, Jabo and Fiona tried their best to reassure him that no one was after him, but he didn't believe them. James also mentioned that he couldn't go back to Earth because it was even more dangerous there. He was so frightened he just stayed curled in a ball, watching with vigilance and sobbing all the while. Then after a calm injection, he fell asleep on the floor. He has since been unreceptive to going out and about or talking to anyone."

"This is awful!" August declares, "It's utterly crazy!"

"I know." Awe's eyes fill with sadness as he adds, "but that's not all. Um. One of our Guides was also affected by this."

Evangeline cannot believe what she is hearing. "A Guide? How is that possible?"

Guides as their title implies are there to guide souls and must always do so with wisdom, patience, compassion, objectivity and a clear head. Happy Juice would not be conducive to their objectives.

Awe explains that one of the Guides, someone named Elliot was having a difficult time as of late. "You see, one of his charges was struggling more than usual on Earth and no matter what he did, he couldn't comfort them or impulse them to make a positive shift. Things were looking pretty hopeless."

MacGregor nods knowingly. "Been there, done that, got the T-shirt." Just as the words came out of his mouth, MacGregor's Hawaiian shirt temporarily swaps itself out with a T-shirt that says 'I'm having a bad day today. I could use a hug".

Awe continues, while fighting back the urge to embrace everyone. "The idea of sitting down to a Contract negotiation and getting someone else he cared about to sign up for Earth again, seemed overwhelming to Elliot. He admitted how he was feeling to his partner Guide Stan before their meeting started. Elliot then suggested that he would only need one little sip to get through it. Stan obviously discouraged him from drinking Happy Juice and recommended a postponement until he felt better."

"Unfortunately, Elliot was not convinced, and before Stan could stop him, he took a gulp of the stuff. Elliot's response was a mix of sadness and fear. He quickly became totally inconsolable and was unwavering in his determination to never send anyone to Earth and watch them suffer ever again."

"As with the others, a calm injection was administered, and Elliot was less upset. But Elliot is currently incapable of fulfilling his Guide duties. He has also been seen sitting silently by water for long stretches of time just watching waves roll in and out to shore. And if anyone approaches him, his eyes go wide and he starts to tremble."

"Oh man, that is horrible," August blurts shakily, thinking if had he had eyes in his head, they would be gushing tears at the moment. "I can now understand why you guys characterized this as a level 5. This is bad. Really bad. We need to get this under control right away. Can I safely assume that all administering of Happy Juice has ceased until our investigation is complete?"

Awe nods vigorously. "Oh yes, definitely! And all Contract negotiations have been postponed until further notice."

"Good. Good," Evangeline says.

"Have you gathered and locked up all the containers of Happy Juice that are in question?" August then asks.

"Yes, we have," MacGregor proudly chimes in. "The kegs and even the glasses from which everyone drank have been stored away for analysis."

Evangeline's face relaxes with relief at what she is hearing. "Excellent."

August starts to bounce around the room in some regular pattern almost as if he were pacing. Evangeline asks him to settle in one spot because he is making her nervous. He tries, but his own nerves get the best of him. In an effort to keep focused, he asks, "Has the Happy Juice Distillery been informed yet?"

Awe squirms in his seat. "Yes and no" he says worriedly.

"Uh, what do you mean yes and no?" Evangeline asks with alarm in her voice.

Awe reminds Evangeline and August that all of this mess occurred just the other day. The Contracts department has been up to their non-existing eyeballs with trying to do everything they can to stabilize the situation on their end.

He assures them that they were able to briefly reach out to a contact at the Happy Juice Distillery about a potential concern. However, they didn't have the time or opportunity to give them all the information, not that they had all the information at the time. They really didn't know the full extent of the issue until late last night when the Distillery was already closed. And of course, their priority was to meet with PS first thing in the morning to figure out how to proceed and hopefully bring this nightmare to an end.

Evangeline asks August to flash over to the Distillery immediately and have everything shut down until further notice. She also directs him to begin setting up interviews with employees and schedule the PS's tech team to begin a thorough analysis of the facility.

After August leaves, Evangeline informs Awe and MacGregor that she will be having some of her staff come by shortly to pick up the Juice for analysis. She also requests that they provide her with a list of everyone involved, so that she can have her team conduct more in-depth interviews and full energetic evaluations where applicable.

Awe practically leaps from his seat as he realizes he forgot to mention something important.

"What is it?" Evangeline asks.

"There is one more thing, um. Unfortunately, it makes this case even more confusing than it already is."

"What's that?"

Awe once again hesitates to even say it. "Not everyone who drank Happy Juice responded unexpectedly."

This time Evangeline almost falls out of her chair. "What? How is that possible?"

MacGregor offers his theory. "I think it means that either two different Happy Juices were administered or there's some unique variance in the souls who responded normally."

Evangeline feels both impressed and slightly sick at the same time. "That's very astute of you MacGregor. But I have to tell you, this doesn't make my job easier. Even so, I promise you, we will figure this out no matter what's going on."

Awe has no doubt that Evangeline's team of fixers will do what she promises, but he's concerned about what they might discover when they do. "It's clear something is wrong with the Happy Juice," he says in a way that feels like he's trying to convince himself of something. "Well at least it seems as if the Juice is to blame for this craziness. But the real question is how did this happen?"

"More importantly," MacGregor wonders out loud, with a strange chill running up and down his not-truly-physical spine, "Why?"

All three exchange a look between them that says they aren't completely sure they want to know.

MacGregor and Awe express their gratitude and embrace Evangeline in a hug before they all say their goodbyes and begin the task of solving the mystery of what happened.

BACK AT THE RANCH

Evangeline returns to her office to find everyone buzzing about the new problem request.

"Ok everyone" she calls out, "gather around."

Light bodies and physical form carriers alike converge in the center of the main office area to hear their co-worker speak. Evangeline gives her team a brief synopsis of what they know so far. She then alerts them to the fact that this will be an all-hands-on-deck request and all other issues will have to wait until this one is resolved. After making a few initial assignments, she tells the others to stand by because a lot more is coming.

Strong as a Bear and Bob are tasked with labeling and picking up the Happy Juice from Contracts and delivering them safely to the lab. Evangeline delegates responsibility for preparing the labs for testing to Abe and Patty. Juan and Li Li are charged with extracting and labeling samples from the Distillery's five tanks and then bringing them to the lab. The job of locating and creating the necessary spaces where interviews and evaluations will be conducted is assigned to Vigo and Ernst. Bella and Woodrow are asked to track down all the specialists and equipment required to evaluate Happy Juice samples and all the souls who may be relevant to the case.

Meanwhile, Evangeline decides to reach out to a contact of hers who participated in the initial creation of Happy Juice so many years ago. He carries the moniker of Doctor Benjamin, but everyone just calls him Doc B. Doc B isn't someone who is easy to track down. He flits across multiple regions on many planes of reality on a regular basis doing research that is vital to his development of key technology on the Other Side. He also co-runs an important healing facility that works with both Other Side and Earth inhabitants.

You heard right, someone who is alive on Earth can temporarily visit the Other Side, and may do so, for a wide range of reasons. One of the biggest motivations is healing. Souls may choose to travel via their dreams to the Other Side to take advantage of its vast offerings. Doc B's center is a popular option among Earth's residents.

Evangeline knows Doc B could be vital to bringing this issue to a speedy resolution. The problem is finding him.

Evangeline heads back to her desk and switches on the communication device that sits in the rightmost corner of her tabletop. It looks like a videophone or computer monitor with a camera that people might use to Skype with on Earth. But on the Other Side, there are no wires, circuitry, cables, networks, electricity, satellites or batteries required to make it all work. Connections are made through intention, thought and frequency.

You are probably wondering why communication devices are even necessary when souls can interface with one another through telepathy. Telepathic communication is certainly an option, but it comes with certain issues. While there's no need to be in the immediate vicinity of the soul with whom one wishes to connect, the locations involved may help or hamper the process.

The further away someone is from their target, the harder it becomes to aim one's thoughts. Greater distances require greater strength of focus to direct messages. Having to cross different planes of existence can be particularly challenging. This is why many Other Side residents choose to use communication devices. These gadgets, if you will, contain technology that helps focus, stabilize and direct thoughts more precisely to facilitate easier and more accurate interactions with others.

Evangeline initiates contact with the Mind Matters Healing Institute, which was founded by Doc B nearly three centuries ago. The screen lights up. The image of a boyish looking, smiling face appears before her.

"Evangeline, what a lovely surprise!" he says with a sparkle in his spectacle-framed hazel eyes. Since no one requires any aid to their sight on the Other Side, one could probably assume he just likes the look of them. "What can I do for you today?"

She smiles. "Hello Fredrick. I hope you are having a wonderful day."

"I am. Thank you. What about you?"

"Well," she begins with some hesitation. "We have a bit of an issue on our hands that requires some delicacy and expediency."

"I see. May I ask the level of this sensitive matter?"

Evangeline sighs. "Yes, well, yes. Um. It's a level 5."

"Oh dear! Really? So how can I help?"

"I need to find Doc B," she states simply.

Fredrick starts to laugh. "Sorry, couldn't help myself. Unfortunately, what you desire dear sweet Evangeline is going to be quite the challenge to achieve. We haven't seen him around here for at least a year, maybe close to two. I'm not sure."

"Doesn't he check in with some sort of regularity?" she asks as her right foot begins to nervously tap against the floor. Ironically, the rhythmic clicking noise she makes with her heels sounds awfully close to an SOS message in Morse code.

"He checks in here and there," Fredrick explains, "but there is nothing regular about him. We can go for months without even a peep. Truth be told, back in the 80's, we went years without any word. I'm trying to recall the last time we heard from him. I think maybe it was six or seven months ago."

Evangeline closes her eyes and lets out a long sigh of frustration. "Did he happen to say where he was when he last checked in?"

"Give me a minute," he asks, "let me see if I can find someone who knows something."

After a few moments pass, Fredrick returns with a satisfied looking grin. "I just talked to Lydia. She was the last one to speak with Doc B. Lydia says it was actually eight months ago and that he was doing research in the Jaylon corridor of plane 3. He was working with someone named O-bray-em or something like that. Anyway, she said he planned to be there a little while longer and would be heading to Fen in plane 4 as soon as he could. I know he might not be at either place at this point, but it's a start don't you think?"

Suddenly Evangeline feels much more hopeful. "Yes, it is. Thank you so much. Take care, Fredrick."

"You too. Good luck!" And with that, their connection ends.

Using the find option on her communication device, Evangeline proceeds to initiate a locator scan for Doc B's soul in both Jaylon and Fen and some of the surrounding areas in plane 3 and 4. She also creates a search request for someone name O-bray-em in or near Jaylon. The scans will take some time, so Evangeline decides to check on her team's progress and prepare a checklist for the tasks ahead of them.

Just as she is about to go over her list one more time to make sure she didn't miss anything;

Evangeline is startled by Fredrick's sudden appearance. Now standing at the edge of her desk, wearing a white lab coat with clipboard still in hand, he smiles and says, "Sorry. I didn't mean to give you a shock. I found something out that I think might be helpful."

Evangeline looks up at him and asks, "What is it?"

"Remember that fellow O-bray-em I told you about?"

"Yes?"

"Well, that's his name for sure. My assistant Orvillia confirmed it and then informed me that this guy is somewhat of a legend in healing circles. She called him a revolutionary genius and said he could easily give Doc B a run for his money. At least that's her opinion. She went on and on about how the Archives are brimming with information about his brilliant discoveries, inventions and healing protocols."

"Orvillia also told me that he is known to travel a bit like Doc B. She then happened to mention that he has a huge lab complex in Jaylon at which he is said to prefer to spend most of his time. So, finding him should be fairly easy. And when you do, I'm sure he'll be able to help you track down Doc B."

Evangeline practically leaps up from her seat to embrace Fredrick in one of the most crushing hugs he has ever had. "Thank you! Thank you! Thank you!" she shouts, still holding him way too tight for comfort.

His face flushes red from either embarrassment or the sheer discomfort of being embraced too forcefully. "So happy I could be of assistance," he says with a strained voice and wobbly smile.

Evangeline finally realizes she is practically choking him, and suddenly releases her grip. "Sorry."

He loosens the tie from his neck and waves his hand. "No need. No worries." Fredrick suddenly realizes he has to be back at the lab for a meeting and says "Got to go! Good luck!" and then disappears with a giant poof.

Just then, an image of a stunning dark-haired male with blue green eyes pops up on the screen for Evangeline's communication device. Her energetic heart flutters, while a blend of sheer peace and joy flows throughout every level of her being.

The smiling face before her belongs to her long-time love Ellery, whom she has been dating since the 1950s and has shared many lifetimes with on Earth. He is the cookies to her milk, the cheese to her pizza dough and the water and sunlight to her flowers. Ellery is her perfect partner and someone who always makes her be and feel her best.

Let's be clear, he never answered to that name when he lived on Earth. You see, just like Evangeline, he chose something that he wanted to be identified by that made him feel more like himself. He played around with a few different names for a couple of decades, and then finally settled on one that would eventually stick. For some reason, the name of a quirky character in the campy 1970s TV mystery series called "Ellery Queen" really spoke to him. So, Ellery it would be.

Ellery works in the Inventiveness department in Science City Center (SCC). His team is responsible for coming up with new objects and ways of making the human experience easier and then planting the idea into someone on Earth to produce. That is not to say that all great ideas that are implemented on Earth come from the Other Side, but a lot of them do.

Portable hairdryers, chocolate made into chips, sticky notes, TV remotes (non-voice activated), battery operated toothbrushes, frozen soda pop machines and USB flash drives are among Ellery's most notable accomplishments. His most recent achievement enables automobiles to parallel park themselves. Evangeline thinks he's brilliant and one of the most handsome, kindest, funniest and creative souls she knows. For Ellery, the feeling is mutual. He is Evangeline's biggest fan and cannot imagine floating around the infinite Universe without her.

"My darling love," he says in a voice that sounds like the most beautiful music to her not-truly-physical ears. "Are you having a good day?"

"Oh Ellery," she practically coos, "dearest sweetheart, I am having quite the day. I cannot say that it is good, but things are looking up."

"Pray tell?" he asks. "Did your team get a meatier assignment like they were hoping for?"

Evangeline laughs. "You could say that. We have a level 5 on our hands."

Ellery nearly falls over. "Holy smokes! Level 5!"

"I know" she says nodding and somewhat smiling. "And you are going to like this part," she adds. "There's a bit of a mystery involved."

He claps his hands in delight. "Awesome! I'm on the case. Let me be your Ellery Queen or Watson!"

"Alright Mr. Queen-Watson, don't get ahead of yourself. We'll talk later when I get home."

"Shall I take something out from the Nostalgia café? Maybe some Pizza or southern fried chicken and biscuits?"

The Nostalgia café is a popular dining establishment in the EW that manifests cuisines and beverages from all regions and cultures on Earth. It gives Other Side inhabitants an opportunity to have something from their old lifetimes. It also allows souls to try things from more modern eras out of pure curiosity.

The café prides itself in being able to recreate dishes from virtually any time period. Whether it's a meal that dates back to ancient Greece or something far more contemporary, Nostalgia makes whatever Other Side inhabitants may crave. While the food and drinks don't taste exactly like their Earthly equivalents, they are pretty darn close. As such, many souls will take advantage of the unique and satisfying opportunity it provides at one time or another.

Ellery and Evangeline are frequent diners at the place, as are Awe and MacGregor. Aside from his love of sweets, MacGregor is what one would call an aficionado of all things noodle. Be it beef stroganoff over buttered noodles, Chinese Ramen or Lo Mein, southern macaroni and cheese, Jewish noodle pudding, Pad Thai, German spaetzle or good old Italian spaghetti and meatballs, MacGregor is always open to chowing down on some of his favorite pasta creations. He is quick to point out though that the long, julienned strips of zucchini that present-day Earthlings call "zoodles" are not, nor will they ever be a noodle to him. So, don't even try it.

"That will be wonderful Ellery," Evangeline says, "but I think I'm more in the mood for lasagna or fettuccini Alfredo."

"Yum! Do you want garlic bread with it?"

"Of course. And don't forget the tiramisu for dessert."

Ellery's mouth curves down into a frown as his hand dramatically clutches at his chest. "You wound me my love. Me forgetting something sweet for my sweet. Impossible!"

"I'm sorry" she says with a giggle. "I didn't mean to offend your character or your incessant sweet tooth. I really must run now. See you later!"

"Ciao bella! Ti amo!" he says waving vigorously before the screen goes blank.

After she disconnects from her communication with Ellery, Evangeline hears a distinct gagging and kissy noise running over and over in her head. She turns around to see August's glowing self hovering behind her.

August continues to make noises and then mimics her and Ellery's voices in her head. "I love you. No, I love you. You're so beautiful. No, you're beautiful. Oh Brother! You guys make me want to hurl if I had a stomach and mouth. I mean seriously get a room!"

"You're just jealous!" Evangeline proclaims with a scowl on her face and her hands planted firmly on her hips.

"Am not!" he declares more defensively than usual.

"You are. You are also a big old scaredy cat! If you ever let down that wall of yours, you might find someone who could make you happy and fill you with love. And when that happens, you will proudly say gaggy things all the time and bring your heart's desire lasagna, garlic bread and tiramisu to make them happy. And you know what else? Doing so will make you even happier."

"Humph! Not going to happen. No siree." And just to emphasize his point, August lets out one of the longest and loudest burps Evangeline has ever heard. Thankfully, he didn't follow up with one of his famous silent but deadly smelly farts, because from what she has heard, they are not easy to recover from.

Evangeline shakes her head. "Alright, August, enough is enough. We have a level 5 to resolve. Let's get back to work. Do you have a status to share?"

"I do."

"And what is it?"

"First of all, the Distillery is now shut down until further notice. Juan and Li Li have already extracted samples from all five tanks and dropped them off at the lab that Abe and Patty have wonderfully readied for testing. Strong as a Bear and Bob have picked up and labeled all the Happy Juice and glasses from Contracts and dropped them off at the lab."

"Utilizing information provided by both Contracts and the Distillery," he continues, "I made a consolidated list of everyone who will need to be interviewed and analyzed. Speaking of which, Vigo and Ernst have already made significant progress with respect to the spaces for conducting our evaluations. And Bella and Woodrow have secured much of the equipment required and are steadily tracking down the specialists we will need for our investigation."

Evangeline is somewhat surprised by how much has been accomplished and how quickly. "Wow, that's impressive!"

"Just doing our jobs."

"And as usual, doing them well," she adds with a radiant smile. I have some news on my end as well." Evangeline proceeds to tell August about her checklist and update him about the Doc B situation.

"That is a really good idea!" he says truly meaning it. "I totally forgot about that guy. If anyone can crack this, Doc B can. While you do have some leads, I wouldn't get too stuck on the idea of us finding him quickly though. Hopefully, we will get this tied up in a bow very soon without him."

"I hope you're right. By the way, I'll need you to head up the interview team. Recruit anyone who you think will be up to the task. And please start scheduling interviews as soon as you can. Abe and Patty will be organizing and helping conduct lab tests, while Bella and Woodrow will be coordinating all energetic and spiritual evaluations. Everyone else will be helping where they can. I would like to have a meeting to analyze findings at the beginning of each day until this is resolved."

"Okey Dokey," August says with a mental image of a salute in Evangeline's head. "Just so you know, however, I will not be able to attend tomorrow morning's meeting."

"Why not?"

"My mother Grace is passing over and naturally I'm on the welcome home committee."

After someone dies on Earth, spiritual helpers will guide them to the Other Side. Once there, they will be greeted by loved ones who have passed before them. They will also be met by their Guides and Guardians, as well as some of the souls they knew in other lifetimes. This celebratory reunion of sorts begins a soul's transition to life on the Other Side.

"Had she been ill?" Evangeline asks.

"Not really, but time has taken a toll on her heart. Tomorrow it just gives out."

"I see. Is your father, um, well…?"

"Dad is still alive. He's really going to struggle without my mom. Quite frankly, I suspect it won't be too long before he joins her here."

"I imagine that you are right. So, have you decided if you will be coming as you are or?"

August interrupts her. "I am going to look like she last saw me. The way I looked before that stupid shrimp dish killed me."

"It's been 35 years August. The shrimp dish didn't mean to kill you nor did the chef who prepared it. It was an accident."

"I know that. Anyway, you know how this goes. It will be a lot easier for Mom to see something familiar when she first gets here. Speaking of which, my grandmother and grandfather are coming and so is my Aunt Sarah. That's her sister."

"How lovely for you all."

"Yeah, it should be pretty nice. Boy, I haven't seen my grandpa and grandma since I crossed over."

"Why has it been so long?"

"My grandparents are super busy and so am I. Don't forget, they have been here a lot longer than I have. Let's just say, they have their regular schedule and aren't eager to change it much. Besides, they died when I was really young, so we didn't have a lot of time together to bond. And that was the only lifetime we ever shared. Anyway, as for Auntie Sarah, she and I get together pretty often. You would love her. She's a riot."

"I would like to meet her," Evangeline says.

"She would like that too. I've told her a lot about you and the work we do. She is super intrigued by it all."

"Does she carry a physical form, or does she do the light orb thing like you?"

"Auntie Sarah has chosen to move about with a body representation like you. She loves the versatility it presents. I don't think I've seen her with the same haircut and color twice over the years. Her fashion also changes all the time. But otherwise, she looks exactly like she looked when she was twenty-five on Earth, except she's a bit thinner."

"So, what are you wearing?"

"Definitely a suit. Mom loved it when I was dressed up, which was pretty rare for me. Special look, for a special lady."

"Awe."

"My mom was one of the smartest and nicest people I have ever met. She was truly an inspiration to the students she taught over the years and has been the biggest inspiration in my own life. She always encouraged me to follow my dreams and be my best. And she was the kind of person who just made the world a little bit better by being in it."

"She sounds amazing."

"She was," August says wistfully. "She was there, you know."

"Where?"

"My exit moment. She attended my ceremony and rooted me on like a super fan. Then afterward she joined me and my colleagues and friends at a celebratory luncheon. It kills me that she saw me kick the bucket. Aside from having my life cut short again, it was the thing that made me feel the angriest when I got here. I never wanted to cause my mother any pain. She did everything for me and was everything to me. She didn't deserve that."

Evangeline notes some shakiness in August's words. "I'm so sorry," is all she can say.

"Thanks," he says while making a mental note about how glad he is that he doesn't have visible eyes, 'cause he would be crying like a baby.

"Well enjoy your reunion. Take as long as you need. Take the day off if you like."

"Thanks. That's not necessary. The morning should be fine."

"Alright, but if you change your mind."

"Ok. Have to go schedule some interviews. Ciao bella!" Then with a little giggle August disappears in a flash.

SOME LIGHT DINNER CONVERSATION

Evangeline starts to set the table on the back deck in preparation for when Ellery comes home with their dinner. The rear of their house overlooks one of the most beautiful expanses of water and is backdropped by some of the most majestic of mountains. The vista is truly breathtaking.

Remember, it's all about choice on the Other Side. How you look, what you do and even where you hang out or live is all up to you. Just like food, no one needs a structure in which to live, but many choose to dwell in one. Because there are unlimited choices and no constraints, you can choose any size and style of house and furnish it any way you wish. You can also place it in any environment that appeals to you.

Evangeline's best friend Annabelle, for example, feels happy in a standard two-story brick colonial with shutters and little to no front porch. She's also not big on land, and thus has very little of it. Her co-worker Strong as a Bear absolutely loves his teepee. Of course, it's a lot bigger than the one he lived in on Earth. It also has more luxurious furnishings, as well as deluxe amenities like a 3-story stone fireplace and an attached stable and pasture for his horses. The teepee also has a retractable sky light, through which he can view the stars. He was also firm about installing windows to let in lots of light and a pleasant breeze.

Abe, another co-worker, lives in a fairly rustic cabin in the woods with scaled down offerings. Except for the Olympic size pool that occupies the entire back end of the property, that is. He's been known to say that if he doesn't get in his daily lap, he won't be good for anything.

As for Evangeline and Ellery, an old white farmhouse with a wraparound porch suits them perfectly, along with lots of land and a view of the sea and mountains. The water was a must for her, while mountains were a necessity for Ellery. Of course, both agreed that their front porch had to be lined with rocking chairs so that souls who came to visit them could linger there. It was just the right thing to do. And if they served their porch sitters ice cold lemonade while they hung out for a while, all the better.

After indulging in a lovely swim at Abe's house, Evangeline and Ellery recently decided to add on a pool to the side of their home. When she was last on Earth, there were only swimming ponds nearby. And in earlier lifetimes Evangeline only swam in the Ocean and a few lakes here and there. The concept of a pool was completely foreign to her. But once she tried it, she was hooked.

Ellery on the other hand, was very familiar with pools. Both he and Abe explained that on Earth they generally had strong chemicals added to make them clean and safe to swim in. Abe and Ellery were overjoyed with being able to swim without the stinky, eye-stinging stuff. Evangeline is grateful she will never know the difference.

She looks down at the results of her efforts and smiles. The simple long wood table is beautifully set with shiny white plates trimmed in gorgeous peacock blue to match the cloth napkins that are folded beside them. Crystal goblets with silver trim and perfectly polished silverware complete each setting. A delicate silver candlestick stands gracefully between them. The flame of the blue candle it holds, flickers orange and gold and will continue to burn until she intends it to be otherwise. A fragrant mix of brightly colored flowers arranged in a simple blue ceramic vase also adorns the table.

The sound of waves gently lapping against the shore and going back out to sea create a soothing environment, as does the music that plays softly in the background. Evangeline takes a seat and simply gazes out across the water while she hums along to the tune and peacefully waits for her dearest love to return with their food.

She didn't have to wait too long before Ellery pops into the dining area of their home and calls out to her. "Where are you?" he yells.

"I'm out here," she yells back.

In just a moment's flash, Ellery suddenly stands before her carrying two large bags in his hands. Each is imprinted with the Nostalgia Café name and the catch phrase, "Food that takes you back to the good old days".

"I hope you are energetically hungry," he says with a grin. "I couldn't decide between fettuccine Alfredo and lasagna, so I got both. I also picked up some cannoli as well as the tiramisu you asked for. And for some extra indulgence, they stuffed the garlic bread with gooey cheese. Can you believe it?"

Evangeline can't help but laugh. Goodness gracious she adores that man.

After a delicious, groan-inducing meal, Ellery and Evangeline conjure up one of the most beautiful sunsets. Pink, purple, orange and blue now swirl above the mountains and streak across and reflect off the water below. The candle on the table still burns brightly as does the firepit that is perched on the strip of beach that borders the deck. Evangeline and Ellery are stretched out in two cushioned lounge chairs that sit partially sunken into sparkling sand. Music still plays softly in the background.

"Mmmm," she murmurs while gazing out at the spectacular array of color and light in front of her.

"I second that," he says. "I hate to disrupt or even ruin the gloriousness of this moment, but I'm near bursting with curiosity. Are we going to talk about your latest case?"

She smiles. "Of course."

Evangeline proceeds to catch Ellery up on all the details she knows so far, as well as what they are doing to resolve the situation. He listens intently, while his not-so-tangible eyebrows and mouth adjust accordingly in response to some of the more interesting pieces of information.

"Well," he finally says. "You know, if I didn't know any better, I would swear this is a story someone made up for entertainment purposes like they do on Earth. It's pretty crazy."

"I know. Even ever stable and cranky August is noticeably shaken by all of this."

"Can't say that I blame him. This isn't the norm for the Other Side. Not even close. So, have you considered whether or not this was accidental or intentional?"

Evangeline nearly falls out of her chair in shock by Ellery's question. "You don't mean to say that you think there is any possibility that this could be sabotage?"

He shrugs. "It could be."

"If this were Earth sure, but here on the Other Side, I just don't feel like it even warrants consideration."

Ellery pats Evangeline's hand. "I know it's troubling to think of such a thing occurring here, but you and I both know it's possible. Souls are souls.

They are not perfect despite these near perfect surroundings. And my dearest love, because it could happen, you need to allow for and investigate all options."

"I know Ellery. We will. Gosh, I really hope what we find is simply a case of someone making a mistake."

"Me too," he says with a nod. "But if it's not a mistake, perhaps we should discuss possible motives."

"Yes, I think you're right. It may help me to see how plausible it is for someone to intend disruption or harm."

Ellery begins listing off possibilities. "Maybe it's someone who works at the Distillery who doesn't like their job."

Evangeline rolls her eyes and shakes her head. "No, I don't buy it. No one needs to work here; let alone at something they don't like. If they are unhappy, they can quit."

"I hear you," he says nodding. "What about someone with a grudge? Perhaps they were targeting another soul who was planning to return to Earth at the same time they were intending to return. What if they wanted to get back at them for some reason or even prevent them from going back to earth?"

"Interesting," Evangeline says with a faraway look in her eyes. "I guess revenge is possible. But this sort of thing requires a lot of planning and... Anyway, even if someone wanted to, how could they swap out the Happy Juice without anyone noticing?"

"They could have help," Ellery offered.

"Are you saying a Guide could be involved?"

"They could, but there are plenty of other souls who have access that are not Guides. And it's not like there's been a big concern over security before. So, really anyone could have had the opportunity to do something."

"True. Ok, what are some of the other motives?"

"Maybe someone has something against one or more of the Guides involved. This could be a setup."

"That's cold," Evangeline proclaims with a shake of her head. "I just don't think that scenario holds much water. Souls don't have to go to Earth, nor do they have to have the same Guide every time. And even if someone did want to get back at a Guide, why now?"

Ellery sighs. "Good question. And while I see your point, remember souls are imperfect and emotional. Thus, they are totally capable of doing something that defies reason and logic. Granted there are far more positive conditions here, but not all baggage is left behind when a soul gets here. Case in point, August."

"Yes, I know. But despite August's luggage so to speak, he would never do anything to hurt someone here just because of something that happened in his past."

"That my dearest Evangeline is because his soul has a deep, core need to serve and protect. I'm sorry, but not everyone shares his values or beliefs."

"You're right."

"On a lighter note," Ellery says with a grin, "maybe this whole thing started because someone has issues with beverages on the Other Side in general. I for one was extremely disappointed in the chocolate milkshake I had the other day."

Evangeline laughs. "That may be so, but I do not recall you sobbing or shrieking in terror or trying to get back at the souls who served you because of it. So, no I don't think that's it. I would also like to point out that you usually order your milkshakes with malt. This time you had it without any."

"Oh, you're right," Ellery says excitedly. "No wonder it didn't taste as good. Promise me you won't let me do that again."

"I promise."

Ellery suddenly looks serious. "I hate to say this but maybe it's someone who doesn't want people to go back to Earth in general. I mean, it can be awfully unpleasant there and everyone who had the negative response to Happy Juice was adamant about never returning."

"I would say that's a bit extreme. However, I know we can't rule it out. I just hope that's not it. As I said, I really want to believe this was all just one big mistake."

"I as well, but we have to prepare ourselves for both scenarios. I for one am super curious to see what the lab tests reveal."

"Yes, me too. So enough about all of this. Tell me about what's going on with you."

"As you know," Ellery says with a frustrated exhale, "I've been between projects as of late and appear to have a creative block of sorts. Nothing seems to be coming to mind."

"Don't worry, you'll think of something soon. You are brilliant and it wasn't that long ago when you were in your groove figuring out how to make a car park itself, especially parallel parking. Speaking of which, I've heard it can be quite the nightmare to accomplish without help. Needless to say, I hope you are not simply wallowing and obsessing. Please tell me you are keeping busy and doing something constructive to distract yourself?"

"As a matter of fact, I am currently helping others prove out their ideas before they can be given the go ahead and downloaded to Earth. It's keeping me out of trouble, and I would have to admit some of it's pretty fun."

"Good! Anything really cool you could tell me about?"

"I'm sorry Evangeline. You know that what I do is all hush hush, especially when it's someone else's work. I can't mention anything until they are approved. But I will say, two of the projects I'm testing are knock-your-socks-off amazing. Just wish I thought of them myself."

She flashes him a mischievous smile. "Maybe you should stick one of your notes to your forehead that says, 'Think of something amazing!'"

"Ha Ha. Speaking of amazing, I just remembered, the Rat Pack is playing at the Stage tomorrow. Frank and the boys are promising a great show."

Evangeline's facial expression shows excitement then quickly shifts to disappointment. "Oh, darn it. I wish I would have known sooner. I would have gotten tickets. I am sure every seat is already spoken for."

Ellery gleams as he informs her, "Turn that frown upside down my darling, for I have tickets. Four of them to be exact. Two for us and two for Annabelle and George. They are totally on board, by the way."

Evangeline practically leaps up from her seat, upending a side table in the process, along with the beverages that rested on it. "Woot! Woot!" she shouts as she shakes her booty and pumps her fists up into the air. "Stand up you stud and give me a kiss!"

Eager to comply with her demands, Ellery jettisons himself out his chair and sweeps Evangeline into his arms. He then dips her in the same dramatic way one would see in an old Earthly movie dance scene. Once he brings her upright again, Ellery plants a long, dramatically loud smooch on her lips and they both break into uproarious laughter.

After they resume sitting, Evangeline asks, "Ellery darling, when was the last time we attended something at the Stage?"

The Stage Theatre, by the way, is a highly popular entertainment venue just outside the EW. It's a place where souls go to witness amazing performances from souls who previously entertained others on Earth. Shows can be dramatic, comedic, and/or musical. They can feature a single performer, a group or even a large Broadway-like cast. Some are intimate affairs, while others are full-on extravaganzas. Regardless, events at the Stage are typically filled to capacity, and always make for a wonderful experience.

While pretty much anything can appear at the Stage, there is one exception. Plays, alleged to be written by Shakespeare can only be acted and viewed at the Other Side's recreation of Earth's historic Globe theatre. The impeccably reproduced structure happens to be next door to the Stage and is regularly packed with fans that span hundreds of years. All plays are magnificently performed by some of the most notable Earthly actors on a regular basis.

Alleged? Contrary to general belief, Stratford-Upon-Avon resident William Shakespeare was not responsible for the literary masterpieces for which he's been given credit.

You see, Will was basically the front man for these extensively studied and performed works. While he offered up his name and helped make productions and publications of the material a reality, he was not their original author. Philosopher, scientist, essayist and statesman, Sir Francis Bacon was in fact the true creator of one of Earth's most famous writings. Although he chose to keep it a secret on Earth, here on the Other Side, however, he has no issue with letting everyone know it.

Ellery and Evangeline love music and theatre and are thus frequent attendees of performances at both entertainment sites. Crooners like Frank Sinatra and his famous Rat Pack buddies are a particularly popular draw for the Other Side, especially since they normally appear only once or twice each year. As a result, getting a seat at one of their shows is usually difficult to impossible. Ellery pulled off a real coup by securing four tickets.

"I think it was about a month ago when Jim Croce played," Ellery finally answers.

"Yes, you're right. What a spectacular concert. I love his song, 'Time in a Bottle'."

"Me too. It's beautiful. But I have to say, 'Bad Bad Leroy Brown' is awesome too. Good beat. Hey, speaking of good music, I heard a rumor that John Lennon and George Harrison of the Beatles are trying to put together a show for later in the year."

"Really? That will surely be an event."

"Yeah. I heard they are planning to expand the Stage for that one night to accommodate the numbers they expect."

"That's probably a good idea," Evangeline says before she clasps Ellery's hand and adds, "Thanks again for getting us seats for the Rat Pack."

"My pleasure. By the way, Annabelle and George will be meeting us there. Do you want me to come to your office or do you want to meet us at the Stage?"

"With what's going on, I probably should just meet you there, just in case I have to cut it close in time." Evangeline's facial expression suddenly turns to worry.

"Sounds good. Listen sweetheart, everything will be alright."

"I know. Thanks."

THE INVESTIGATION BEGINS

The office is bustling with activity. Today is a big day. Lab tests and interviews begin. Hopefully, answers await the team very soon.

Evangeline sits down at her desk to check her messages. Amazingly, she has only two of them. One is from her boss and the other one is from the Distillery. Her boss Vivian is just checking in for an update. She was out of the office yesterday and is eager to find out what is happening. A representative from the Distillery simply called as a courtesy to make sure Evangeline's team has everything they require for their investigation.

After Evangeline delivers the shocking news about their level 5 situation to her manager, she proceeds to check the progress of her scan requests. Sadly, nothing has turned up yet.

Undeterred, she decides to put a call into the Archives to get some information on O-bray-em and his lab complex in Jaylon. She hopes to get some direct contact coordinates and bypass the time-consuming search process altogether. With fingers crossed, Evangeline enters the coordinates and waits for someone to answer.

A smiling, female face, crowned in red curls appears on her communication device's screen. The face leans in presumably for a better look. Big blue eyes stare curiously as a soft lilting voice asks, "Is that you Evangeline?"

"Yes, Viola, it's me. How are you doing?"

"Fine. Fine. And you?"

"Good. Listen, I need to track down some famous healing dude from Jaylon. His name is O-bray-em. He supposedly runs some lab complex over there."

"Are you telling me you never heard of him before?" Viola asks with just a smidge of judgment in her tone.

"No, sorry. I suppose you, on the other hand, are quite familiar with this soul."

"This guy is a legend, a genius and a true innovator! Because we have so much data on him, the Archives dedicated a whole section to him. As for the famous lab complex where he makes miracles happen, he calls it 'Therapeauo'. The word has Greek origins. It means to heal, cure, serve and restore health. And that, my dear Evangeline, is what this guy does on a daily basis."

"Impressive. Do you happen to have the contact coordinates for Therapeauo?"

Viola's head nods as a big grin spreads across her face. "I do. Just give me a minute."

A few moments later, Viola is back with the information Evangeline needs.

"I can't thank you enough. This will be immensely helpful."

"We aim to please."

"And you do. Really Viola, you are a treasure."

"Awe thanks. You too, Evangeline. Is O-bray-em critical to solving your next case?"

"He might be. I am hoping he can get me in contact with a colleague of his who is far more elusive."

"Who's that?"

"Doc B."

Viola laughs a little too loudly. "Good luck with that. He is like a ghost."

Evangeline lets out a frustrated sigh. "Don't I know it. But I am hoping to catch a break here."

"I hope you find them both. Take care."

"You too." And with that, their connection ends.

Evangeline plugs in the coordinates Viola gave her into her communication device. Although she is reaching across to another plane it takes just a moment to connect.

An unusual figure appears on Evangeline's screen. The surface of their skin is purple with fluorescent blue undertones. Their eyes, nose and mouth are narrower and quite a bit smaller than a human's. Imprinted in the center of their high forehead is an ornate pattern of squiggly lines. And where there would normally be hair, a sparse amount of thin black spikey strands protrudes out the top of their head. In contrast to their unique and colorful features, their clothing is quite ordinary and plain and covered in a crisp white jacket that looks like a lab coat.

Thankfully, the translation module on Evangeline's device allows her to understand what the soul on the other end is saying. "I am Lana-ray-so," the purple being says. "How may I be of assistance to you, faraway Miss?"

Evangeline clears her not-truly-tangible throat nervously. "Yes, well, my name is Evangeline. I am calling from the Problem-Solving Department on the Other Side. I am trying to locate O-bray-em. Is he there by any chance?"

"Oh no, Miss. The O-bray-em is on a research mission. He is not expected to return for quite some time. Can someone else at Therapeauo help you?"

"How long would you say he will be gone?"

"I cannot tell you."

"Is he in contact with you? I mean, can someone contact him where he is?"

Lana-ray-so shakes her purple head. "Sorry Miss, but no one can reach him at this time."

"I see. Is there someone at your lab complex who has worked with Doc B that I may speak with?"

"One moment Miss, while I check for you."

Evangeline's fingers drum nervously on her desk while she waits. *Darn, darn, darn,* she thinks. *This is going to be a dead end. Ugh!*

Lana-ray-so comes back with her head bowed low. "I am so sorry Miss. The ones who know Doc B are with O-bray-em. No one who is here now has much familiarity with the fine gentleman."

"Would you know if Doc B left any contact information with your facility?" Evangeline asks now grasping at straws.

After taking a moment to check, Lana-ray-so returns and shakes her head. "Once again Miss, I am sorry. The only information he left with us is his own lab's coordinates on the Other Side."

"Well thank you anyway. Have a lovely day."

"You as well Miss."

After the connection ends, Evangeline feels a tremendous urge to hit her head repeatedly against the top of her desk but thankfully resists the impulse. It's not often that she could even come close to succumbing to discouragement, but something about this case is really bothering her. "This is day one of the investigation," she reminds herself out loud. "Get a grip, suck it up, put your big girl panties on, and go investigate!"

"Talking to ourselves, are we?" her co-worker Abe asks with a mischievous grin.

Her betraying face turns red with embarrassment. "Yeah, well. What's it to you?"

Abe chuckles. "Wow Evangeline, I haven't seen you like this before. You do know that we're going to fix this. This is what we do. Sure, there's a lot more at stake here than usual. But we will be victorious."

"I'm glad you think so," she says with a little too much snark. "Oh, I'm sorry Abe," she adds feeling guilty for her attitude. "Perhaps the Alfredo didn't agree with me."

"Huh?"

"Never mind. Do you have any status or updates I should know?"

"Nope. Just noticed you were talking to yourself. Just wanted to see if..."

"Alright, well. Let us get back to work."

"Yes boss."

A few hours have passed since Evangeline came into the office. She's been making the rounds at their lab and interview locations and talking on her communication device the rest of the time. Abe suddenly approaches her desk.

"May I have a word?" he asks.

"Of course. What I can I do for you?"

Abe smiles. "I wanted to tell you that we have already discovered something interesting."

Her gaze locks on Abe's face. "Yes, what is it?"

"From what we can determine, it appears we have two versions of Happy Juice reserved in the Distillery's five tanks. Three of the tanks have the same makeup, while the other two share an entirely different identical composition. The juice held in three of the tanks are a perfect match to samples taken from Contracts that are believed to be tainted because of their undesired effects."

"Really? What about the other two tanks?"

"The contents of the two remaining Distillery containers, presumed to be untainted, match up to some, but not all of the Contract specimens that are assumed to be uncompromised.

"What do you mean by some?"

"Yeah, that's the strange part," he answers with a truly perplexed look on his face. "Some of the samples taken from Contracts that yielded a normal response, ended up being an exact match to the two Distillery tanks we assume to be good. Unfortunately, some of them are an identical match to the three other tank samples that are thought to be corrupted."

"Well that certainly gives us more questions than answers," Evangeline says with some degree of uneasiness in her voice. "Although we cannot be certain, it does appear that only some of the Distillery

Juice was contaminated and only a portion of Contract's reserves were infiltrated with the unknown agitating component."

"Yes, we believe that is a good assumption. But while determining how much was compromised is helpful, it isn't as high a priority as understanding why souls had both normal and undesired responses to an obviously altered Happy Juice."

"I agree. Have you uncovered what the contaminant is yet?"

"No. That's going to take a lot more time. We are just measuring similarities and differences at this point in our analysis."

"That was highly informative. Thank your team for all its hard work. Let me know when you know something more."

"I will. See you later."

Abe walks away while Evangeline jots down some notes about what they discussed.

A hush suddenly comes over the place as a tall, blond haired, blue-eyed, bronze-tanned man in a dark gray, pinstripe suit steps through the door. Latin music begins to play in the background. The mysterious visitor starts to rhythmically move his hips, feet and arms to the sexy beat of the song while traversing through the main office area.

Everyone is seemingly mesmerized by the sight before them. No one can look away. "Who is he?" they whisper excitedly among themselves.

"It's me!" he announces, as he raises his arms in the air and continues to sway and gyrate to the music.

Evangeline stares in shock as she recognizes the voice immediately. "August? Wowzah!"

"Yeah, pretty amazing huh?" he says in a way too cocky voice. "And you thought MacGregor and Awe were something. How 'bout this?" he asks while pointing his thumbs toward his chest. August then proceeds to shimmy with his palms facing upward while slowly turning around to reveal his shaking, taut booty.

"Not bad," Evangeline says with a grin, all the while doing a thorough top to bottom assessment with her very surprised eyes. "Not bad at all. It pains me to admit it, but you were a tall drink of water on a hot sunny day dude!"

"I know, right! Thought I'd show you all what you have been missing before I go back to my light body." And with that, he transforms back to his hovering light-ball self and the Latin beat is gone.

"Thanks for that," Evangeline says still shaking her head and smiling.

"Don't mention it," he says in her head. "Truthfully, it was more for me than all of you. I guess I needed to know that I still have it."

"You have nothing to worry about. So how did things go with your mother?"

"Wonderful really. It felt so good to be with her again. She was so happy to see me and know that I was alright. My grandparents were really sweet and of course my Aunt was her usual funny self. It was also a treat to see my old dog, Ollie, again and actually know what he was thinking and saying. He is one funny dude. All in all, it was a great reunion. Lots of hugs. Lots of laughs. Even a few tears. Tons of stories. There were also a few surprises."

"Really, like what?"

"Well, you know, if they're available, souls from her other lifetimes may come to the welcome home party. I had no idea that Mom had lives in Atlantis and Ancient Egypt. I also hadn't realized she was a healer and a scientist in many lifetimes and accomplished many wonderful things. She also had a bit of the royal in her, which in retrospect I can totally see. And I don't know why I never made the connection before, but Mom was that Russian defector's mother when I was a British intelligence officer. When she discovered her daughter was killed, she died of a broken heart. Katia, that's the name of the Soviet agent who died with me. She was at the party. Can you believe it?"

"Wow, very synchronistic. But the timing with your mom is off. In linear years, she couldn't have come back and be old enough to give birth to you."

"Yeah, I know. Stupid parallel lives. Time isn't weird enough, so let's create multiple versions of it."

"Ugh, I agree. So, what's Katia up to these days?"

"She does soul rescue."

"Impressive. Really important stuff!"

"Yeah I know."

Soul Rescue (SR) is a department located in HQ center. As its name implies, the primary purpose of its team members is to rescue souls who have become trapped or lost. As you know, some souls may miss their opportunity to cross over to the Other Side after passing and can become stuck in an in-between plane of existence.

The in-between is not conducive to comfort or peace and can easily and unnecessarily extend a person's suffering from their Earthly lifetime. It can also have adverse effects on the living and the Earth plane itself.

Because they don't belong there, efforts are made by departed loved ones, Guides, as well as SR agents to move these stuck individuals along. Of course, having some intuitive person on Earth perceive them and send them to the light also works. Unfortunately, most people view these entities as something to be frightened of, so the benefit of them having a psychic gift is typically lost.

Aside from missing one's transition window because of choice or confusion, souls can also become stuck or lost in other ways. For example, all too often, a soul may choose to journey to or simply drift into an undesired region within the vast multidimensional Universe. What many do not realize is that some of these areas can be fraught with danger due to the presence of darker or more negative energy and influences. SR workers bravely help lost or stuck souls essentially find their way home no matter what the circumstance may be.

You could almost see the wheels turning in Evangeline's head. "I imagine she has some interesting tales to tell."

"I'm sure she does."

"Do you think you'll see her again?"

"We um, have a date," August admits hesitantly.

"Really. How nice for you."

"Don't read too much into it," he cautions, while he nervously bops up and down in the air.

"Never," she says waving her hand his way. "Just try to have a good time."

"I will."

"So where are you taking her?"

"Don't laugh."

"I won't. I promise."

"She wants to go to the Nostalgia café and then watch a movie."

Evangeline laughs despite her promise not to. "Does that mean you are going to take on a more physical form for said date?"

"Yeah. That's what it means."

"Does she know um, that you typically don't?"

"Oh yeah, of course. But I can do the physical thing here and there. Besides, Mom was talking about bagels and pizza and shrimp and chocolate cheesecake this morning and it just got me kinda wanting some."

"I better sit down before I faint," she says as she plants the backside of her hand against her forehead.

"Next thing you're going to tell me is that you're going to take up basketball or tennis at the Athletic Club in the EW."

"Nope. Nothing like that. Just a nice evening with two souls who want to catch up. And definitely a piece of cheesecake. Maybe some popcorn with the movie."

"Uh huh. Speaking of movies, do you think they'll ever come out with National Treasure 3?"

"I hope so and I know I am not alone. The series has a huge following on both the Earth and the Other Side. No one seems to know why it hasn't been produced. And let's face it, that Cage dude is not getting any younger, so they better hurry up."

"I agree. So, Katia… It's interesting that after all this time she comes back into your life because of your mom. Did you happen to have other lifetimes with her?"

"Yes, three more to be exact."

"Really?"

"Katia was my sister during our first life together. Then she was my husband. And finally, in the life before our most recent incarnation together, she was my mistress. A mistress, I might add, whom I truly loved but couldn't be with in a more formal sense due to social status and all that stupid class stuff."

"Two lifetimes as lovers. Oooooh."

"Shut up."

"Make me."

"Humph! I told you not to read into this."

"I know what you told me but… So, did you and the Soviet agent ever take your relationship to a more romantic level before you both met your demise?"

August pauses a little too long before trying to answer.

"I see."

"You see nothing."

She laughs. "Let us agree to disagree."

"Humph."

"You know August, in all seriousness; I really do hope you have a lovely time. I am also incredibly happy to hear your reunion with your mom went so well."

"Thanks. So how are things going here today? Any new developments?"

The conversation quickly turns to all business. After Evangeline fills him in on the latest, August heads off to check on the progress of his interview team.

Just as August leaves, Juliette, another PS team member approaches Evangeline's desk. The stunning dark-haired, dark-skinned female could easily give Evangeline a run for her money in both the looks and fashion department. The woman also happens to be brilliant. "Do you have a minute?" Juliette asks.

"Of course, what is it?"

"Just wanted to let you know that we closed the "intermittent Lifetime Review device failure" case today."

A Life Review, by the way, is conducted sometime after a soul returns from a life on Earth and prior to them going back again. Some choose to do it soon after crossing over to the Other Side. Others may opt to wait closer to the time they are set to enter a new lifetime. Regardless of when they do it, the purpose of a Life Review, as its name implies is to objectively evaluate a soul's last life on Earth.

With the help of their Guides and Guardians, a soul will compare what they set out to accomplish in their Contract to what they actually achieved or experienced on Earth. Together they will determine what went right and what went wrong, as well as how things might have been done differently and perhaps for the better.

Life Review devices allow souls to view scenes from their former life that are relevant to the discussion at hand. These glimpses offer different perspectives and generally promote greater understanding. The devices also enable viewers to know what everyone in the scene was genuinely thinking and feeling for expanded context and awareness.

Through this process, souls can actually feel both the positive and negative repercussions of their actions and words upon others. To know how much comfort and joy one has given someone or the difference one has made in somebody else's life is a wonderful thing. On the other hand, becoming aware of and understanding the more hurtful impact one has had can be quite difficult. Doing so, however, is not intended to be a judgment or punishment, but rather an opportunity to learn from one's mistakes.

Personally experiencing the pain one has caused often fosters greater personal responsibility, as well as feelings of remorse and a desire for forgiveness. It could also be a powerful motivating force for someone to strive to do better for others and themselves in future lifetimes.

Unsurprisingly, Life Reviews are also an essential input to the Contract negotiation process. They help a soul and their Guides develop new objectives and strategies for their next lifetime by taking into consideration what happened in their prior one. The hope is that with the knowledge, understanding and advice coming out of their Life Review, a soul will improve upon what they did before. Unfortunately, it doesn't always work out that way.

"You did?" Evangeline says excitedly. "Excellent! What did you find out?"

"The source of the issue came from a nearby experimental lab," Juliette explains. "Apparently, they developed a new piece of equipment that emits unusual sound waves that can cause an unexpected and immediate disruption to the signals received by Lifetime Review devices. Because they did not run this new bit of technology on a regular basis, the disturbance caused to Lifetime Review devices was intermittent."

"Two things have since been done to resolve the issue," she continues. "New shielding has been added to all viewers to protect them from any intrusive streams. The lab in question, more importantly, has installed special protective linings throughout their facility to neutralize the waves being produced. This will eliminate any potential for their emissions to do harm to anything or anyone within or outside of their location."

"Great work Juliette! And what a fascinating reveal."

Juliette smiles. "Thanks."

Evangeline shakes her head. "I have to say though, it continually surprises me how much goes on here that I haven't a clue about and how complex things can get."

"I know."

"By the way, I love your dress! Such a gorgeous green."

"Thanks. I manifested it from a couple of items I saw in an Earthly fashion magazine recently. Anyway, now that I'm free, do you want me to work in the lab or help with interviews or energetic evaluations on the level 5?"

Evangeline thinks for a moment. "Actually, I'd love it if you would check in with the lab and also help out with energetic evaluations when you can."

"Will do. Catch you later Evangeline!"

DARKNESS IN THE MIDST OF LIGHT

At the farthest end of the EW complex is a large cluster of buildings referred to as the Infirmary. The Infirmary is where souls go to heal.

Sometimes the degree of trauma a person undergoes on Earth is so great, their soul will require an extended period of rest and healing upon passing over to the Other Side. That is not to say that everyone who has experienced physical and/or emotional trauma will require recuperative time or healing when they arrive at the Other Side. The Other Side is nonetheless prepared should the need arise.

While physical discomfort and ailments leave a soul immediately upon crossing over, the more mental and emotional wounds do not. Oftentimes, therapy and curative energetic protocols are necessary to aid souls in better understanding and dealing with what has occurred. The vast treatment offerings of the Other Side can also enable someone to mend their spirit, recover their strength and peace, and eventually move forward.

The Infirmary is subdivided into areas based on symptom severity and the degree of care required. Of all the sections, C deals with the worst cases. Charles is a healing specialist who works in Infirmary C. He's been helping souls recover from some of the most horrific experiences on Earth for at least a century. His area utilizes multiple Other Side technologies along with therapeutic discussions to help souls overcome the trauma they carry. Infirmary C currently has twenty-six patients in process. The following are examples of some of the types of cases they deal with.

Chin-Mae was born in a small village in communist North Korea. He was a bright, loving and joyful boy who spread kindness wherever he went. Also highly curious, he observed everything and everyone around him and always had many questions for the people he encountered. Many of them thought, too many questions. He saw things that did not make sense to his logical mind and even more so, that caused his empathetic heart to hurt. As such, unlike his quiet and meek parents, he felt the need to speak out about widespread injustices and the numerous restrictions of his people's liberties.

Like his name, which means truth, he felt compelled to tell the truth about what was going on and bravely challenge the powers that be. The ruthless leader of his country was not at all pleased about the dirty laundry of his regime getting out into the world. He viewed Chin-Mae not only as an agitator but as an enemy. Therefore, like many others, Chin-Mae was imprisoned, starved, tortured and made to watch someone he loved tortured and killed. And then when he could bear no more, he was ultimately silenced for good.

Needless to say, his experience left a deep scar on his soul that would need some time to heal. Thankfully, he would not take as long to recover as others who've made the Infirmary their temporary residence. Feeling very encouraged by his quick and steady progress, his healing team expects him to be able to leave treatment within the month.

Zora, whose name represents daybreak or sunrise like the time of day she took her first breath, isn't doing quite as well. She was born into a strict Muslim family in the country of Afghanistan. Her father and mother subscribed to the highly oppressive, discriminatory, restrictive and often barbaric Sharia Law. Combined with the patriarchal domination that's particular to Islamic culture in the Middle East, Zora would never be truly free. She would never look the way she wanted or have the option of wearing what she wanted. Nor would she ever be able to learn what she wanted or even say or do the types of things she wanted. Also given that she was female, she would always be regarded as inferior or nothing more than a second-class citizen.

While Zora was not inclined to complain or challenge the ways of her people, she was nonetheless unhappy about the extreme unfairness of her circumstances. Regardless, she did her best to keep herself out of notice, let alone trouble, and always did what was asked of her. She even agreed to marry a man that she didn't like, let alone love, because it was expected of her.

One day, as if life wasn't difficult enough, something terrible would happen that would ultimately cause Zora to lose her life. When a highly regarded member of her village brutally raped Zora, she could no longer stay silent. She told her husband and her parents what had happened and even alerted the governing authorities, hoping for justice.

Unfortunately, the law states that she is required to have four male witnesses confirm her alleged rape. Without that type of testimony, she would be considered an adulterer and sentenced to death. Naturally, there were no witnesses. And the repulsive man she accused called her a delusional liar and pathetic woman who dishonored her marriage and chose to blame someone else for her ungodly ways.

It wasn't a big surprise that no one believed her. Of course, the law was also the law. Therefore, poor Zora was stoned to death by her community. Even her own parents and husband threw jagged rocks to mar her body and cause her to bleed. It was the ultimate betrayal and unfairness. As such, even in the safe and loving haven of the Other Side, Zora could not overcome what she endured. It was just too much to bear. She arrived inconsolable and although she has found some relief in the month she's already spent in the Infirmary, she still has a long way to go.

Then there's Ellen. She lived her whole life in the mid-west of the United States. Ellen came from an extremely poor family. Sadly, her father got hurt at his job early on and couldn't work. The small amount of money he received for his injury wasn't enough to support a family of five easily. Her mom was neither highly educated nor skilled, so the only job she could get to help provide for her family was to clean other people's homes. It was hard work and didn't pay very much, but it kept them from living on the streets.

As soon as Ellen was old enough, she picked up a parttime job after school, working in a local grocery store. Every penny she earned went to help her family.

When Ellen turned seventeen, she met a boy named Ray, who was too handsome for his own good and knew it. Ray took a liking to Ellen and decided she would be his. She was more like a prized possession he needed to acquire than someone whom he cherished and loved. He was obsessed and relentlessly pursued her until he wore her down and she finally agreed to go out with him.

They dated for six months before Ray proposed. Naïve and desperate to leave her home, Ellen agreed. Her parents told her she was too young and should wait, but Ellen was stubborn. Despite her family's objections, Ray and Ellen eloped and moved to a bigger town where he would build his fortune.

It didn't take long before Ellen found herself living in a large, fancy house and having anything she wanted at her disposal. Life had suddenly become easy. Ray was pulling in so much money from all his schemes and investments; she eventually quit her job and became a fulltime housewife. Not too long after, Ellen became pregnant and eventually gave birth to a son. Then a year later, she had another child, a baby girl.

As time went on, Ray showed less and less interest in her and her children and preferred to spend his time out with his buddies and business associates. There were also lots of other women. Ellen couldn't say or do anything to stop it. And as much as he had the freedom to do what he wanted; Ellen was not afforded the same flexibility.

Jealousy and possessiveness fed Ray's need to control her. And when his luck seemed to finally run out and their finances took a big hit, things got even worse. Stress, worry and self-doubt fueled his anger. Before Ellen knew it, she began to bear the brunt of his frustration and insecurity with frequent beatings and demeaning barbs. The constant physical, emotional and verbal abuse she endured eventually took its toll. Fear had taken hold and she felt neither the confidence, courage, nor power to do anything to change her circumstance.

Then one day, Ray came home so drunk and enraged, there was no way to reason with him or calm him down. Without provocation, he grabbed Ellen roughly and started to punch her repeatedly until she collapsed onto the floor and could barely move. While she lay there bloodied, bruised and sobbing, he ran out of the room and returned with their two small children and a rifle in his hands. Her son and daughter were crying and visibly confused and scared.

Before she could even say his name, Ray shot their son first, then their daughter. Ellen screamed and cried and struggled to get up. Before she could even reach him, he shot her dead.

Ray is still alive on Earth but has managed to escape authorities thus far. Although Ellen was reunited with her children on the Other Side, the shock, anger, confusion and grief she felt before her passing would not subside. She was practically catatonic upon arrival and has shown little shift in the two weeks she's been in the Infirmary.

Her most coherent moments are filled with shrieks of terror and anger, and of course crying. Her children are in a lot better shape than she is, but they will need some time to be fully stable. The Infirmary's staff has arranged a few visitations between them each week in hopes that it will help. Unfortunately, Ellen is too confused and upset to recognize them as real events versus delusions of her broken mind. So, the work will continue.

After Infirmary healing specialist, Charles, finishes making his rounds for the day, he wraps up everything and gets ready to head home. While no one typically experiences things like fatigue, stress or overwhelm on the Other Side, Charles has never felt wearier than he does now. He is also extremely sad. It is a despair that is all encompassing, like a dense dark cloud that has enveloped his entire being. No matter how hard he tries, he has not been able to break free from it and connect with the light that is so abundant on the Other Side.

Although the stories he listens to each day are not easy to hear, Charles has always been able to sustain his cheeriness and hope, despite them. But as the days continue to drift by, it has become a struggle to even muster up an occasional and brief smile.

He chose the work he does, because his soul has always been empathetic to the suffering of others. Serving to uplift and bring peace and comfort to those who need it most has brought great joy and peace to Charles' own soul. At least, until recently that is.

Unfortunately, discouragement has begun to take root. Any fulfillment he used to experience from facilitating and witnessing someone's shift from pain to ease is becoming more elusive. Going to the Infirmary is getting harder with every day that passes.

Charles has seriously considered leaving it all behind, but something inside of him does not appear to be ready yet. And so, he continues to plod forward and show up at a place that is increasingly dimming his light force.

Charles arrives home to his thatched roof, quintessentially English stone cottage and takes a seat on a swinging bench at the edge of his exquisite garden. He is surrounded by lush greenery and a spectacular array of colorful clusters of flowers and plants. There's also a weeping willow tree that stands adjacent to a lake that sparkles as the light hits it. The serenity and beauty of the landscape typically has a soothing effect on him, but not today. All he can feel is despair and anger.

His longtime love Debra shares the home and garden with him. She arrives shortly after he does and joins him on the bench. Debra immediately senses his sorrow and gently takes hold of his hand. She then leans toward him, rests her head on his shoulder and closes her eyes. Her soft, golden brown hair brushes up against the side of his face like silk.

"Tough day?" she asks.

"Mm," he murmurs in response.

"Want to talk about?"

"Not really."

"Do you know what I have in my pocket?" Debra asks playfully coaxing him to guess.

"No. What?"

"Two tickets," she says, lifting her head to flash him a glorious smile while holding up two fingers in the air.

"Tickets?"

"Yes. We my dear sweet Charles are going to see the Rat Pack tonight!" Her hazel eyes now glimmer with joy.

"I don't know Debra," he says in a trembling voice, "it's been a long day and..."

"And nothing. Listen Mister, we are going! You need this. I need this."

Debra, by the way, works in the Science Center as a researcher in the Science Archives (SA). Coincidently, she knows Ellery, because he frequently checks out information from the SA that may be relevant to his inventions.

Debra has observed a steady decline in Charles over the course of nearly a year. She has tried everything she could to uplift and distract him. She thought an evening out at a show would be just the thing to cheer him up. But something that would normally make him jump at the chance appears to be more overwhelming to him than anything. Debra is extremely worried. Her typically fun-loving guy is slipping away, and she doesn't know how to stop it.

"I don't mean to be a downer," he says with a sigh. His blue gray eyes seem to get grayer as he speaks. "I'm not trying to be difficult."

"Oh honey, you are not difficult. You just need to do something to get out of this funk you're in."

"The uplifting effect of a show is only temporary Debra. It doesn't change your life. I still have to go to work tomorrow."

"You don't have to go. You can quit."

"That's what my therapist says, but I can't quit. Not now. Souls need me."

"They will still be helped Charles, just not by you. You have helped so many souls over the years. It's time for you to help yourself."

"I know that you're right, but…"

"But nothing. You are coming to the show with me tonight and we are going to have a fabulous time. Then tomorrow, I will go with you to the Infirmary and you will submit your resignation and that will be that. I think once you are free of work, you and I should take off for a lovely adventure somewhere spectacular. Time and distance, not to mention, a good deal of fun and relaxation should help you recover your joy-joy and balance again. I just know it. And if you are honest with yourself, you know it too. Please tell me you'll do what I suggest."

"Alright Debra. I will."

Debra feels as if a big weight has been lifted.

"Thanks for loving me and being here for me," Charles says, gently touching her cheek with his hand.

"Oh Charles, it's the only thing I can do. There is nowhere I would rather be. My heart belongs to you."

He embraces her in his arms. "As does mine to you," he says as a single tear slides down his not-truly-physical cheek from his not-truly-physical eye.

"Everything will be ok," she whispers as she nuzzles his cheek.

Charles isn't quite sure, but he is finally ready to take a leap to see where it will lead him.

IT'S SHOWTIME!

Evangeline quickly puts her things away for the day and then manifests a full-length mirror before her. She needs to figure out what to wear for the evening. Just like an Earthly girl, she changes her outfit at least five times before settling on one. "That's it!" she finally exclaims as she turns and shifts to get a good look at each angle. Evangeline is decked out in an exquisite full length, sleeveless, v-neck, emerald green sequined gown with matching high-heel pumps.

"Now the hair," she says out loud before instantly transforming her jet-black locks into a formal updo, adorned with just a few delicate rhinestone pins.

"Hubba, hubba!" she hears in her head.

She turns around swiftly, causing the bottom of her gown to swirl a bit. "August? You're still here?"

"Yup. Just doing some prep for tomorrow. You look O-mazing!"

"Awe thanks."

"Where are you going?"

"The Stage. We are going to see the Rat Pack."

"Excellent! I saw them last year. It was incredible." August bops up and down a few times just to emphasize the point.

"Did you go to the one where Judy Garland popped in to perform with them?"

"Yes. It was so cool. You know, it's really interesting to me how much better everyone sounds without all the booze, drugs, smokes and emotional baggage they had on Earth. Not that they sounded bad with them. But whoa, tons better without, you know?"

"Yeah, I've noticed that too. Very interesting. I am so excited for tonight."

"Well, I hope you guys have a good time. Are Annabelle and George going with you and Ellery?"

"Yes," she says proudly, "Ellery picked up four tickets."

"That's great."

"So, when are you and Katia taking in a movie and hitting the Nostalgia Café?"

"In a couple days. She has to finish up a few things before she can be free."

"Have you figured out what movie you are going to see yet?"

"Movies," he corrects.

"Movies? You're seeing more than one?"

With the enthusiasm of a teenager, August explains, "Like duh! Originally, we were only thinking of watching the last three Star Wars movies. Then we decided to do a complete marathon of every Star Wars related film, including 'Rogue One' and 'Solo'. And we plan to do it in the sequence of the story's timeline versus when the films were produced."

"Star Wars huh? Why Star Wars?"

"Star Wars," he states with almost reverence, "has everything. Good vs evil, adventure, space travel, spiritual wisdom and truths, the 'Force' and light sabers! The films are a cornucopia of goodness wrapped in a complex study of human behavior. It's one of the finest representations of Earth's ultimate challenge despite it not taking place on Earth. Do you choose the dark side or the light? Good stuff. Good stuff."

"Of course, the Harry Potter series," he continues, "offers a lot of the same things Star Wars does, only they use wands instead of light sabers and everything takes place on Earth. Now while they don't refer to the 'Force' per say, they certainly touch on the power of love versus hatred and fear. Not to mention, how much they emphasize the whole concept of how it's all about our choices. So, after we get through our Stars Wars Marathon, we will be taking a plunge into the wizarding world."

"Wow! You are deep August. I have to say though, it's going to take a long time to get through all that."

"So? Time is irrelevant here."

"I know, but even so, it's not like you'll be able do it all at once without any breaks for work or anything else."

"We figure we'll do one or two every day until we get through it."

"That's a lot of time you will be spending together."

"It's a commitment yes. But both of us think Star Wars and Harry Potter are worth it."

"Just Star Wars and Harry Potter?" she asks with a smirk.

"Evangeline."

"August."

After a long silence, Evangeline asks, "where are you watching all of these films and are you doing take out from the Nostalgia or having popcorn every time?"

"Katia has a huge movie theatre in her house that's linked up to the Archives. We are planning to have some Nostalgia café eats and some popcorn but not every time."

"What's her home like?"

"I don't know yet, but she says it's in the style of a Swiss chalet and it has spectacular mountain views and a stream that winds through the property."

"Sounds lovely. I still can't believe you will be doing the physical form thing."

"It's no big deal. And I might not do it the whole time. You better get out of here or you are going to be late."

"Oh shoot! You're right. See ya tomorrow!"

"Have a great time!"

And then with a poof Evangeline is standing outside the Stage theatre.

To add to the drama of the event, a red carpet is rolled out in front as search lights rhythmically flash and cross against the star filled night sky. The crowd, elegantly dressed in tuxedos and formal gowns, is buzzing with excitement as they make their way through the main entrance. The partially opened doors are tall and covered in sparking silver. Each has a face mask etched onto its center in crisp black. One is for comedy and one is for tragedy. Both faces are encircled by musical notes, also colored in black.

As Evangeline makes her way toward the lobby, she spots Ellery, Annabelle and George just to the right of her. They wave and smile and within a few moments she is standing by their side.

Annabelle is wearing a stunning one shoulder, black and white gown with a slit over her right leg. Her golden wavy, shoulder length hair is simply adorned with a single rhinestone barrette on each side. Both men are wearing traditional black tuxedos with matching black bowties and vests on top of crisp white shirts. Thankfully, they avoided tails and top hats because that would have been too much.

Ellery clasps Evangeline's hand and gives it a gentle kiss. "You look absolutely beautiful tonight."

"Thank you," she says with a demure blush, "you look pretty amazing yourself."

Her head turns to her friends. "Actually, all of you look wonderful. It's so fun to dress up, isn't it?"

Annabelle nods. "Yes indeed! I feel like a fairy princess. Ellery, we are so grateful that you chose to include us."

He waves his hand at her. "Tut tut. How could I not?"

George chimes in. "Well we really appreciate it. By the way, I heard from my co-worker Lenny today that there are supposed to be a few surprise guests popping in tonight."

"Really?" Evangeline asks, "Like who?"

"I'm not sure, but he said they may be from one of the movies in which Frank starred."

"That can be anybody" Annabelle says with a frown. "He was in tons of movies."

"More than 70 films," Ellery clarifies.

"I guess we'll have to wait and see," Evangeline says with a smile. "Shall we head inside to our seats?"

Everyone agrees and passes through another set of doors that lead into the showroom. Upon entering, they all feel an immediate twinge of disappointment.

The Stage chose a more traditional theatre layout versus a more vintage-like setting for the evening's performance. Evangeline and the others assumed the venue would be transformed into a replica of the famous Earthly Copa Room, where the Rat Pack frequently played in the 1960s.

The Copa was a popular feature of the historic and long since destroyed Las Vegas' Sands Hotel. Once owned and run by mobsters and even the crazy but brilliant Howard Hughes, it was a playground for the rich and famous. Its showroom was named after the highly regarded Copa Cabana nightclub in New York. The brightest and best talent came from all over to play the Sands. Most revered among them was the Rat Pack which was led by the famous Frank Sinatra.

And while many of his talented friends came to join him over the years, Dean Martin and Sammy Davis Jr. shared the stage with Frank the most. Aside from singing and dancing, audiences were regularly treated to fascinating and funny stories, dead-on impressions of famous people, comical interchange, teasing and jokes, and joyful camaraderie. Many a cigarette and cigar were smoked while copious amounts of alcohol were consumed by both the entertainers and the entertained. A good time was usually had by all.

Strategically and conveniently located next to the casino, the original Copa room contained three hundred and eighty-five seats. Tonight's show, on the other hand, will accommodate six hundred audience guests. The back of the stage has also been extended so the orchestra can be positioned further away and provide more room for the entertainers. Also, unlike the original club where patrons were seated at tables, this evening's attendees will sit in rows of chairs like one would see in a normal theatre.

Evangeline's group finds their seats, which happen to be in the center of the fourth row.

"How did you get such amazing seats?" she asks staring incredulously at Ellery.

He smiles. "My co-worker Eduardo. You see his amore du jour, Alfonso, coordinates events at the Stage. I told him if the Rat Pack ever comes, I would appreciate an early heads up so I can get good seats. He said, 'no problem,' so voila we have spectacular seats!"

Annabelle high-fives Ellery. "You did good Mister! Please convey my deepest appreciation to Eduardo."

"I will. I actually think Eduardo looked at this as an opportunity to thank me. You see, I discovered a flaw in his invention during testing recently that would have caused it to be delayed significantly or even fail approval. So really, he kinda owes me."

"Regardless, he is awesome," Evangeline declares, "And so my dear are you!"

"Oh, look who's here," Ellery suddenly says out loud as another beautifully dressed couple comes their way. "Debra, how nice to see you."

"Ellery," she says, "what a lovely surprise."

"Evangeline, Annabelle, George, this is my friend Debra. She works at the Science Archives and helps me a ton with my research. Debra this is my dearest Evangeline and our lovely friends."

"So nice to meet you all," Debra says practically gleaming. "This is my honey, Charles."

Charles gives a half smile and says a simple, "Hi," while making a tiny wave with his fingers.

"What do you do Charles?" Evangeline asks.

Debra decides to answer for him. "He's been working as a Healing Specialist at Infirmary C for quite some time."

"Wow! That is one heavy duty job you have," Annabelle remarks. "I cannot imagine doing what you do. I'm sure you hear this all this time, but your courage and selflessness are awe inspiring. Thank you Charles for helping souls who cannot help themselves."

Charles is visibly moved by her sentiments and feels a bit overwhelmed. "It's been, well, um, I um, well, thanks."

Debra pats Charles' arm. "He is very loving and brave. He's also quite modest." Eager to change the subject she says, "Evangeline, I understand you work for the Problem-Solving department."

"I do."

"Anything really interesting on the plate these days?"

"Yes, as a matter of fact, we have ourselves a level 5."

"Oh my, that's pretty serious."

"Yes, it is. Unfortunately, I can't tell you anything about it at this time."

"Oh, no worries," she says with a hand wave. "I'm just curious."

Desperate to act normal and change the subject away from problems, Charles decides to offer up some information related to the Rat Pack. "You all should know we have a legit Copa girl in our midst."

Copa girls were beautiful, classy showgirls who entertained patrons of the Copa Room with their dancing.

Ellery's eyes go wide. "Who?"

Debra's face flushes red. "Me."

Everyone practically jumps up and down with excitement at this revelation.

"Did you um work there when Frank and the boys played there?" Annabelle asks.

"I did!" Debra says nodding. "It was incredible."

"Did you grow up in Las Vegas?" George asks.

"Oh no. I was from a tiny town in nearby Idaho. I came to Nevada with a friend of mine to try to make some good money and get some dancing experience. I also hoped to make a few famous contacts. Both of us eventually planned to go to California and try our luck in the movies."

"Did you ever get to California and get your break?" Evangeline asks feeling quite curious.

Debra's eyes turn sad. "Unfortunately, no. I did have a meeting scheduled with an agent I met at the Copa, but I never got there. I was just a few minutes outside of LA when a truck hit my car and I died on impact."

"That's awful!" Ellery says. "I'm sorry."

"It's long ago history now. It's ok. Who knows, I could have been a star."

"You are my star," Charles says sweetly.

"As are you to me," she says touching his cheek.

An announcement over the speaker system requests that everyone take a seat because the show is about to start. "Everyone put your hands to together and welcome to our stage, the Rat Pack!"

Cheers and clapping echo through the large theatre as the stage lights up and Frank Sinatra, Sammy Davis Jr. and Dean Martin suddenly appear waving to the crowd. Each of them looks as they did in 1960s Las Vegas at the peak of their careers. The orchestra starts playing and the three men break into song. Their first selection is "Luck Be a Lady" from the musical "Guys and Dolls". Frank, by the way, appeared in the movie version of the famous Broadway show in 1955.

After a rousing performance, Frank makes some typical introductory statements and thanks the audience for being there. Before they continue with their act, he makes a request to the crowd. "I understand we have some former Copa girls here with us tonight. How 'bout you baby dolls stand up and show us where you are."

Debra looks over at Charles and asks, "Is it okay?"

"Of course," he says. "Do your thing!"

With that, Debra rises from her seat and within a flash is dressed in a stunning blue sparkling sequined costume and head piece, complete with matching feathers. She stands with her hip slightly jutted out to the side and her hands up in the air. She calls it her Ta Da pose. Five other beautiful women pop up in equally impressive costumes and stances. The audience goes wild.

"Now that's what I'm talkin' about," Frank says. "Nice. Very nice. Hey maybe you gals can come up later and delight us with your fine footwork. But until then, let's get on with the show."

Over the course of several hours the audience laughs, cries, sways, sometimes sings along, and simply sits mesmerized by what they witness. It is more than a show. It is an experience. Also, to the delight of everyone, the special guest is Gene Kelly, one of the most beloved dancers of all time. Frank and Gene sing and dance to the song "New York, New York" from the musical movie "On the Town" in which they both appeared together in 1949. The crowd roars and claps so long; Sammy and Dean have to come back on stage to break things up with jokes, so they can get on with the show.

The entertainment ends with an emotional rendition of "My Way", a favorite among Sinatra fans, which he recorded later in his career. Unfortunately, the Copa girls never make it to the stage, but that's alright. No one leaves unhappy. Even Charles feels surprisingly uplifted by the evening's end.

BACK TO REALITY

The conference room is filled to capacity. The morning status meeting is about to begin. "Alright everyone," Evangeline says, "let's all come to order. We have a packed agenda, so let's get on with it. Abe, if you please, give us an update on how lab testing is going."

Abe clears his throat and curves his mouth into a half smile. "Well um, lab testing is progressing. As I've indicated in our last meeting, we have measured similarities and differences that confirm the existence of two versions of Happy Juice. Unfortunately, they also left us more confused about their contradictory effects."

"For something to create both a positive" he says as he stretches out his right-hand in front of him, palms facing upward. "And a negative response," he says now shifting to his left-hand and then pausing for dramatic effect. "There must be something unique about the individual who consumes it, that determines the response they have. We've passed this onto the team who is analyzing the energetic aspects of the individuals involved to see if they can determine the cause for these variances."

"As for identifying the contaminant, we have thus far been unable to determine its exact makeup, let alone origins. Truthfully, whatever it is, it is not something we've seen before."

"Keep at it," Evangeline says. "Hopefully, if we can ever track down Doc B, he might have a clue as to what this mysterious element is. Unfortunately, my scans have come up empty so far, so we'll have to muddle through without him. How are we doing with the interviews, August?"

August flutters up and down a few times before answering. "Interviews are continuing nicely. We've gotten through about a third of the list so far. The team is documenting things as we go and creating profiles of all relevant parties. We are also producing charts and statistical analysis from the information we are gathering, to uncover patterns and motivations that could explain the situation."

"Has anything stood out yet?" Evangeline asks.

"Yes and no. On the surface nothing appears to be out of the ordinary or of much consequence. However, we did notice something interesting regarding a couple of souls who were unaffected by the tainted Happy Juice. When we talked with their Guides, we discovered they both share the same reason for going back to Earth. They also have similar backgrounds and have attained comparable levels of soul mastery and frequency."

"Both of these souls, being extremely advanced and high vibrational, carry little to no baggage from their prior Earthly incarnations. And unlike most souls, their purpose for returning to Earth was not about cleaning up junk or healing themselves personally. Their motivations were of a more altruistic nature. They simply desire to be of service at this critical time for the planet. Both of them want to help facilitate healing and evolution as the Earth's vibration and frequency rises and humans are impulsed toward higher consciousness."

"Mind you, we haven't been able to interview all relevant parties yet to see if this is a consistent pattern among all of the souls who were unaffected. But we see this as an important part of the story. It could very well support the lab's theory about the reaction one has being tied to something that's particular to a given soul versus something external to them."

"Very interesting. Of course, this still doesn't answer how the Happy Juice became compromised in the first place, but it is a vital clue in helping us to understand the conflicting responses. Have you had a chance to interview any Distillery workers yet?"

"We've gotten through a few of them. So far, they all appear to be as happy at their jobs as the juice they produce. Well almost as happy. We still have more souls to speak with. Hopefully, something will shed light on this in a future interview. I'll let you know as soon as we know something."

"Good. Bella? Could you give us a status on the energetic evaluations?"

"Yes Evangeline. Our specialists have thus far identified large amounts of negative emotional debris within the affected subjects' energetic templates. Strangely, the intrusive fragments do not carry origin markers consistent with any of these souls' historical experiences."

Everyone at the table is visibly shocked by the revelation. Evangeline practically falls out of her seat. "Are you saying someone else's proverbial emotional luggage is floating around in these poor souls' beings?"

Bella hesitates to say what she needs to say out loud, not wanting to make it any more real or true than it is. "Yes. Sadly, that's exactly what I'm saying."

"Holy shuzbot!" August proclaims a little too loudly in everyone's head. "Woops. Sorry."

"There's more," Bella adds. "Our specialists believe the junk is comprised of emotional garbage from many souls."

"Oh dear," Evangeline says. "Is there any way to know where or who they came from?"

"We are trying to work on the where, but the who will be near impossible to determine."

"What about the debris itself? Is there anything within it that might lead us to the source?"

"Sorry. Not at this time."

Evangeline looks around the table at her peers. "Obviously, there are few more threads to this mystery we will need to explore before it can be solved. But good work everyone. I wonder, has anyone mentioned to any of you about observing something unusual lately?"

Everyone simultaneously shakes their head and says, "no."

Evangeline finds it odd that no one saw or heard anything out of the ordinary. Obviously, whoever did this was incredibly careful and perhaps brilliant. She can't help but think back to her conversation with Ellery about possible motivations and decides to share them with her team. "I encourage all of you to think about these potentials and let me know what your instincts are telling you."

"I for one," Woodrow admits immediately to the group, "believe this to be intentional. This is far too complicated to be some accident."

Vigo nods in agreement. "Absolutely. I totally concur. Whoever did this, wanted to do this."

Before Evangeline knows it, everyone in the room is saying the same thing. The entire team, it would seem, is convinced that this is a case of sabotage. She didn't want to admit it, but she knew they were right.

"Alright," she finally says, "if this was a deliberate act, we need to understand why. We need to explore every possible motivation and identify those individuals who would have a reason to do such a thing."

"Just so you know," August says, "we are already asking souls how they feel about lots of stuff including Happy Juice, the Contract process, Earth in general and the other souls involved in their Contract. So, unless they are holding back the truth, we should be able to snuff out any wrongdoer."

"I didn't mean to imply that you weren't," Evangeline quickly clarifies. "I have complete faith in all of you. I really do hope whoever did this, did not act out of revenge or for some other unsavory reason, even if it was indeed intentional. Unless anyone has anything else to report, let us disband this meeting and get back to work."

Because no one says anything, everyone goes off to continue their investigation. Everyone, except August. "Penny for your thoughts?" he asks.

"I've been doing this for over one hundred and twenty-five years," she says while briefly closing her eyes and rubbing at her temples. "I have never had a case get to me like this one is getting to me. Moreover, for the life of me I cannot even say why."

"Uh huh. May I venture a guess?" he asks.

"Please do."

"You've been here a while and I don't just mean in the Problem-Solving department."

"So?"

"So, let me ask you something. Why?"

"Why what?"

"Why haven't you gone back to Earth?"

"Well, um. I just. Um. I haven't really seen the need, I guess."

"Come on Evangeline. Honestly, why do you stay here?"

"I like it."

"Who wouldn't."

"I'm not really a fan of…"

"The Earth. Huh. Wonder why."

"What's your point August?"

"You don't want to go back because you don't want to feel that bad again. You don't see the value of going to such a terrible place, even if you learn something or heal some aspect of yourself or a relationship you have with somebody else. You stay, because you have more control and there are far more good things here than bad. And now, something bad is happening in your perfectly controlled world that is a little too close for comfort. It reminds you that Happy Juice is a smoke screen for making souls agree to endure unpleasantries that no one in their right mind would sign up for otherwise."

A chill runs through Evangeline's entire being. It scares her how much his words ring true. Unable to even give voice to her thoughts, she makes some excuse about having to check on something.

"Alright, I'll go," August says, "but make no mistake, this is not just about figuring out who slipped something into the Happy Juice and why. This is about a lot more. That's the part that's putting everyone on edge. We all need to take a good hard look at ourselves and the way things work over here and on Earth and figure out how we are going to go forward."

And with that, August blinks out of her vision to head back to his interviews. Evangeline just sits quietly for a few moments pondering all that he said, before turning her attention to something more productive.

Just as she is about to get out of her chair, Evangeline's communication device alerts her that she has a status message for her scans. She opens the notification and to her surprise and relief, she discovers that O-bray-em has been located. Evangeline punches in the coordinates specified by her scan result. A face suddenly appears on her screen. The man on her display looks like a younger version of the famous Earthly Tibetan Buddhist monk known as the Dalai Lama. His kind eyes crinkle as he smiles and says "hello."

"Are you O-bray-em?" she asks.

"I am. And with whom do I have the pleasure of speaking?"

"My name is Evangeline. I work for the Problem-Solving department on the Other Side. I am trying to track down a colleague of yours, Doc B. I understand he was at your facility not long ago and I was wondering if you by any chance would know where I might find him?"

"Ah. I see your dilemma. He is quite the elusive one, even more so than I am. Unfortunately, we have been out of touch for some time and he did not provide me with his itinerary. Could I perhaps be of assistance in some other way?"

"I don't know," she says. "I am looking to Doc B for his expertise regarding Happy Juice. Unless you are familiar with its components and potential interactions with other substances, I am not sure you can help."

O-bray-em laughs at this point. "Good old Happy Juice. I haven't taken a sip of that glorious stuff for at least three centuries. Now while I do not profess to be an expert about that potent brew of bliss, I am quite capable of performing some analysis if that is what you require. I have familiarity with a great many substances from many dimensions and could help identify something for you if that would be helpful."

"That would be immensely beneficial. Is it possible for you to come to our labs?"

"As a matter of fact, I would say your call is rather serendipitous. I have just finished up my work here, so I could come there right away before I head back to my own facility."

Evangeline breathes a sigh of relief. "Thank you. Thank you."

"You are welcome. Shall I come to your location first?"

"Yes. I would like to brief you on the situation before you conduct your analysis."

No more than a second later, O-bray-em is standing in front of Evangeline with a big grin on his face.

"Thank you so much for coming," she says while outstretching her hand to his.

Evangeline spends some time catching him up on what they know so far. O-bray-em is more than intrigued.

"I am particularly eager to examine the emotional debris your team has discovered," he admits cheerily. "I believe it's the key to cracking this case."

"I shall escort you to our lab and introduce you to everyone, so you can get started. Again, I appreciate you coming to help us."

He bows. "I am actually grateful for the challenge and opportunity."

Evangeline is happy to oblige the man. After dropping him off at the lab, she contacts her boss to fill her in on her very promising update. Then afterwards, she heads over to the interview site to see if she can help. August puts her to work straight away and then continues with his own interviews. Although neither of them mentions their prior conversation Evangeline knows it won't be easy to forget.

EVERYONE IS UPSET

The minute Evangeline gets home, she plops herself down on her couch and turns on a device, which looks remarkably like an Earthly television with a remote. Unlike the viewing options available on Earthly cable TV, there is only one channel she can tune into on the Other Side. It's called the Earth Channel. As its name implies, it lets you view what is happening on the Earth.

These are not pre-recordings but rather, real time glimpses. Viewers can watch and listen in on virtually everything that's going on at the present moment. If someone, however, wishes to peruse something or someone from an earlier day, week, month or year they will have to go to the Archives Library to access that past information.

Earth Channel viewers have the flexibility to customize the content that shows up on their screen.

And although many may tune into the same channel, they can be watching different things at the very same time.

Viewers use their remote to target what they want to watch. For instance, they can specify a location to zoom in on. Their selection can be broad like a continent, country, state or city. Alternatively, they can narrow down their search to something more specific such as a street, address or perhaps a room in a building. Other Siders can even view something out in the sea or under the sea or up in a plane or helicopter. No matter where they choose to focus their attention, the device makes it easily accessible.

From large groups to small, or maybe a particular person, Other Side inhabitants can also specify who they want to view. The device also enables the watcher to obtain updates on certain world events as well as individuals. These views are more like briefings with high-level information rather than scenes playing out at a given moment.

Evangeline tunes her remote into a lovely two-story house on a quiet street in the northern coastal town of Traverse City, Michigan. This popular tourist spot known for its cherries and wine is now the home of her friend Amalia who is currently living as a five-year-old boy named David.

Evangeline first met Amalia about twenty-five years earlier at a murder mystery dinner hosted by her dear friend Annabelle. Amalia had the kind of spirit that everyone wanted to be around. She exuded pure joy and love and was one of the funniest souls Evangeline has ever encountered. The two of them discovered they had a lot in common and eventually became close friends.

Amalia recently decided that it was time to venture back to Earth again to address her long-standing issue with abandonment and fear of loss. Frustratingly, no matter how many times she has tried in the past, she has been unable to overcome it. Her response has always been to close her heart, numb her feelings and disconnect from everything and everyone. Amalia hopes that this lifetime will be different, and she can finally conquer this thing once and for all. Evangeline is in awe of her friend's bravery but is heartbroken from watching her suffering.

At five years old, David has already experienced heart wrenching tragedy. He was only three when his mother died from a freak accident after she slipped and hit her head. His father was so overcome with grief, he disconnected emotionally from everyone including his own children. David's nine-year-old sister Sarah, who was seven at the time stepped up to fill the void and provide comfort to her younger brother and herself. But she was still a little girl and still is.

Sarah and David are like two lost souls in a boat on a choppy sea with no paddle or motor to get them safely to shore. Despite his parents having no intention to abandon him, David feels nonetheless abandoned. He is also tremendously confused. He doesn't really know why his mom is gone or why his dad, who is still there, appears to be somewhere else.

Evangeline watches as David cries himself to sleep and calls out to his mom in desperation. Tears start to run down Evangeline's own face. Unable to bear it any longer, she slips briefly into the little boy's room and pats his head. "Hush now, let yourself sleep. You are loved and everything will be ok," she whispers, before flashing back to her home on the Other Side.

Spirit visitations from the Other Side to Earth, by the way, are a lot more common than one would believe and quite simple to accomplish.

The boy's breathing finally slows, as he drifts off peacefully with a smile on his face. Evangeline punches a number into her home's communication device and rings up the soul of David's departed mother.

"Veronica?"

"Yes, who is this?"

Evangeline explains as best as she can before making a request. "I think it would be helpful if you visited him, at least in his dreams. David could really use some comforting right now. He's so sad and confused, and your husband, well, he's not helping."

"I am fully aware of what's happening," Veronica says with sadness in her voice. "I have been visiting him, nearly every day in fact, and I plan to continue to do so until well… I am also trying to help my husband function better and help our children. You know how hard it is to get through. But I assure you, I won't stop trying. Thank you for reaching out and trying to help my son."

"Your son was/is my friend. I want her, I mean him, to be ok. I didn't mean to imply that… I am sorry for…"

"There is nothing to be sorry about. You are kind, compassionate and caring. Earth is well, difficult. It's easy to get sucked into the despair of it. Take care, Evangeline. We shall pray and hold a space for your friend and my child to get through this and come out the other end with an open heart and peace."

After saying their goodbyes, Evangeline continues to watch David sleep for a while and pray for her dear friend.

Ellery walks into the room. "Hi sweetie. Oh, I see you're watching Amalia. How's she doing?"

"She, I mean he was crying again. I couldn't just let it go this time, so I visited him. I patted his head and whispered to him. Thankfully, he finally calmed down and fell asleep."

"Well that's good honey. I know this is hard. But she chose this. You need to let her do this even if it hurts."

"I know."

Ellery sweeps Evangeline into his arms for a hug, at which point she breaks into loud ugly sobs.

"It's okay. It's alright honey," Ellery whispers as he strokes her head and holds her.

Evangeline starts babbling as she blubbers. Ellery doesn't know what she's saying but he tries to be reassuring, nonetheless. Eventually, Evangeline blurts out, "He's right!"

"Who?"

"August."

"What is August right about?"

"I'm a pathetic weenie!"

Ellery's eyes register shock at Evangeline's pronouncement. "He said that?"

"No," she says with a huge shudder.

"I don't understand Evangeline. Please help me so I can help you."

"I don't want to go back to Earth!"

"Ok, so?"

She looks away in embarrassment. "I never want to go back."

"It's your choice. You don't have to."

"I know, but the reason I don't want to go back is that I'm scared. I'm weak. Oh, and I am also a control freak."

"Hmm. Well, first of all, no one would blame you for being scared. Earth is scary. After all, it's virtually brimming with unfairness, violence, hatred, greed, selfishness, prejudice, stupidity and a whole lot of other unpleasant things. Kindness and compassion are a rarity there, except when something terrible happens and people show these attributes out of fear or guilt. Of course, the minute things change for the better, everyone goes back to their self-absorbed, uncaring selves."

Ellery starts to pace. "And don't forget the lack of justice that exists on Earth. Those who do bad things regularly get away with it and are often rewarded. On the other hand, people who do good things often go unnoticed and unappreciated and are sometimes even punished for their good deeds. That's not to say there aren't beautiful aspects to living on Earth, because there are. Quite a lot of them really. Unfortunately, it can be darn challenging to notice, let alone connect to them."

"As for you being weak," he continues after once again taking a seat. "You are one of the strongest souls I know. I will have to concede however, that you are and probably will always be a control freak. That cannot be disputed. But let me remind you, it's also one of the things that makes you good at your job. And besides, who doesn't like control? I have no idea what August said to you or why you seem determined to beat yourself up. You just need to know that I love you and I am here for you."

"Oh Ellery, I am so lucky to have you."

"I am lucky to have you too. Oh, I forgot," he practically leaps up from his seat. "I brought home chocolate cake from work today. Gary recently decided to move onto something else. Today was his Bon Voyage party."

Before she could even say anything, Evangeline finds herself staring at the biggest piece of cake she has ever seen. "It looks glorious," she whispers, before digging a fork into the mound of chocolate goodness and sticking it into her mouth. The frosting generously coats her teeth and lips and looks absolutely endearing to Ellery as she smiles. "It tastes glorious too," she adds while making groaning noises. "Chocolate cures everything."

"It certainly does my love. It certainly does."

The room seems more crowded than usual. The leader of the group encourages everyone to take their seat. The weekly group therapy meeting for Guides and Guardians is about to start.

So why would anyone need therapy on the Other Side? Well for one thing, souls still have feelings to process through and not everyone requires the intense in-patient therapeutic offerings of the Infirmary. Why therapy for Guides and Guardians? Given the constraints of their job and having to witness suffering on a regular basis, Guides and Guardians are particularly prone to getting upset.

It's extremely hard to get a message through and near impossible to spark inspiration and action in the people they are guiding. While they wait, hope, and pray for some shift, they must watch the people they care about struggle and endure pain. It's not easy and it takes a toll.

Guides and Guardians need some way to deal with the grief and frustration they feel, so they can maintain some degree of stability and do right by their charges. Like brothers and sisters in arms, they need to commiserate with those who understand what they go through. As such, Guide Guardian therapy groups became an essential offering on the Other Side a little over a thousand years ago.

MacGregor and Awe are in attendance, along with every Guide who was affected by the Happy Juice fiasco. That's what they are calling it, by the way. It was decided that such unusual circumstances warranted a special meeting. They considered it particularly critical because of what happened to their colleague Elliot.

The meeting begins with everyone going around in a circle and expressing how they feel about what transpired. Naturally, aside from shock and fear, there is an overwhelming sense of sadness and powerlessness shared by all of them. The uncertainty and confusion about the event in question has also created an unsettling nervousness across the board. But there is something else.

A question hangs in the air. It has been posed many times over the years, but for the first time it seems to be gaining more seriousness and attention than it has in the past. That question is should we still send souls to Earth?

"It is not for us to determine," MacGregor states plainly.

"That may be so," Joanne says as her gaze meets his. "But we need to talk about it. We should also have input on the question. After all, we have to deal with the consequences more than most."

"Yeah, we do," Fiona chimes in.

"That's true," Awe says sympathetically. "But let us not forget, there is good on Earth. And, souls do learn, heal and evolve, even if it takes them a lot longer than any of us would like. There really isn't any better place to test the muster of a soul and impulse them toward change."

"The problem is that change comes from adversity and pain versus joy," Jabo notes.

"It has certainly been the modus operandi from the start of things," clarifies MacGregor. "However, let us remember the Earth has been undergoing a transformation in the past couple of decades that in part, should allow for change to come through something gentler. And as of recently, the results we are seeing are better than anyone's expectation."

"The reports coming out of the Stats department at the EW," he continues, "are showing significant increases in healing activity and evolutionary gains on Earth. In fact, some of us have personally witnessed glimpses of the positive changes that are occurring."

"Why just the other day, Stuart was telling us about how the soul he's been guiding had a major breakthrough. A breakthrough I might add, that didn't seem possible a few months earlier. And didn't Mary brag a couple of weeks ago about a soul she's been guiding finishing the last item on their list of what they set out to accomplish? What a glorious achievement! Progress is being made. Victories are happening. We should be celebrating them."

"I agree," Drake says, "but they occur all too infrequently."

"That might have been true in the past, but…" Awe interjects. "Consciousness and awareness are at an all-time high. At the same time, the vibrational frequency of the planet and its inhabitants are rising significantly."

"Now more than ever, the residents of Earth are being bombarded and impulsed by energies that they can no longer ignore. These energies as you know are intended to bring them to a breaking point that should ultimately cause them to seek out healing and change and make different choices. Choices, I might add, that are better for themselves, others, and the world they live in. As everyone adapts to the changing energies and frequencies on the planet, their experiences can be much easier. And eventually, souls can learn through joy and comfort."

"That all sounds lovely in theory," Joanne remarks. "But humans are stubborn and often stupid. Case in point, people are still killing others in the name of God and religion or hiding behind their religion as they commit ungodly or less than honorable acts. Then there's the countless victims of oppression and/or violence who continue to just accept it and even make excuses for it. And don't get me started about the people who enjoy inflicting chaos and pain upon the world just because they can. Sadly, most of them do these horrible things without even a smidge of remorse. In fact, too many of them seem to relish in others' suffering."

"Let us also not forget how easily Earth inhabitants blame others and never take responsibility for their own words and deeds or the consequences of them. They even have the audacity to complain about their circumstances over and over again and wonder why they never change. Ugh! The pervasive greed, selfishness, stupidity, hatred, unkindness, unfairness and small-mindedness on that planet are becoming unbearable to witness day in and day out."

She blows out a long breath of frustration before continuing. "Innumerable years have gone by and people are still doing the same things they've always done and are dealing with the same lessons over and over. They just don't get it and I'm not sure they ever will. Let's face it, despite all the efforts being made to shift the planet and the whole human race, there is no guarantee that any of it will make much of a difference. How much longer do we hold hope for something better? How much longer do we watch souls screw it up?"

"As long as it takes," MacGregor answers firmly. "It's easy to dwell on the darkness and despair. It's even easier to focus on the failures or disappointments or the yet-to-be accomplished. But there have been so many triumphs, so many reasons to celebrate. Just like the Earthly news, we are only talking about the bad stuff. We are not discussing or even allowing ourselves to discover all the many good things that are happening. The kindness, the compassion and generosity, and even the silliness that people exhibit every day. It barely gets a mention. But that needs to change. And maybe if we start emphasizing the positive, maybe they will too."

After the meeting, MacGregor and Awe sit in silence with heads in hands just staring at the floor. "Well that was fun," Awe says still looking down.

"Yeah, a total riot," MacGregor remarks with a grimace.

"I thought these sessions were supposed to make us feel better."

"They usually do, but these are strange times, Awe."

"They are indeed. Did you notice that our therapy group leader didn't utter a single word during the entire meeting?"

"I did. It was really weird. He just sat there looking ill and shaking his head. I think we broke him."

MacGregor's mouth curves into a half smile. "I think you're right. We need to remember that therapists are people too. It's not always rainbows, puppy dogs and chocolate listening to everyone's problems and gripes all the time."

"Yeah, poor therapists. Not an easy job. No siree. So glad I am not one."

"Totally agree. But you know being a Guide isn't exactly a cake walk either."

"True dat."

"We have so many things that make the job difficult, but lately I've been thinking about one thing in particular."

"What's that?"

MacGregor lets out frustrated sigh. "Sending signs to our people on Earth and having them recognize them as a sign. It's like climbing the tallest mountain in a blizzard. Truth be told, I can't even remember the last time when a plan really came together. Quite frankly, I think I'm losing my touch."

"Dude! You are not losing your touch. You are the man! Your signs are legendary. It's not your fault that some of the souls you guide are thickheaded at times."

MacGregor nods and smiles. "That's true and very therapeutic of you to say. Thanks buddy."

"Don't mention it. Hey, speaking of brilliant signs, do you remember that amazing thing you pulled off at that health food store with Vicky and Elizabeth?"

"Wow, I forgot about that one. It's been a really long time. The store has been closed for more than a decade now and the incident you speak of, occurred at least fifteen years ago."

Awe looks up, smiles, and raises his hands with palms facing upward. "True, but the energy of that shining moment will live on forever."

"Do you always have to be so dramatic?"

"No, but it suits me. Anyway, let us recount that wonderful day when you, MacGregor, Guide extraordinaire, created one of the most envied, spectacular and impossible-to-ignore sign executions."

Amused, MacGregor sits back watching his friend stand before him, speaking of the day in question with as much fanfare as he could muster. Unsurprisingly, Awe chose to use a musical accompaniment to intensify the drama when appropriate.

"It all began on a warm summer's day," he says, as MacGregor could swear he hears the chirping of birds in the distance. "As they have done many times before, dear friends, Vicky and Elizabeth, were rendezvousing for lunch and a long chat. Vicky, being a big fan of its food offerings, suggested that they meet at a small café located in one of the few health foods stores in the area."

"Elizabeth was already seated in a booth when Vicky arrived. After deciding what to eat and putting in their order, they wasted no time at all to dive into discussion. Vicky and Elizabeth are both deep thinkers and are highly expressive in nature, so there was a lot to talk about."

With a more serious look on his face, Awe continues. "While they had much in common, they had different perspectives and temperaments and even a fairly wide gap in their ages. Sometimes that made for disagreement and even conflict between them. But despite that, each of them treasured their friendship with one another. Whenever they did have a negative blip in their relationship, things would eventually return to a more amicable state. After some cool down period, the women would find it easier to focus more on the good stuff and less on their differences and frustrations with one another. It wasn't easy to watch when the two of them were having issues, but it was understandable. They are human after all. And being human isn't always easy."

"Now, part of their differences lay in their beliefs. Both women are open-minded and have explored many otherworldly aspects. Each of these ladies has dabbled in a number of alternative healing modalities that are rooted in energetic, subconscious and spiritual understandings. As one may suspect, this made for some very interesting and philosophical discussions between them. Unfortunately, it also caused them to butt heads."

"Elizabeth is unwavering in her beliefs even if there is no tangible or physical proof for them, or at least something someone else might need to believe them," he states with pride. "Vicky, on the other hand, is open but less inclined to accept things as readily as Elizabeth. She oftentimes dismisses things that bear no logical explanation but are utterly obvious and wonderful to Elizabeth. To Elizabeth's continued frustration, Vicky requires near constant confirmation and reminders to view the magic and synchronicities she encounters as real and valid."

"The type and extent of signs Vicky received compared to Elizabeth also became a point of contention between them. Elizabeth would often say to Vicky, 'You get billboards all the time and disregard them! It's not fair.' The truth is Elizabeth had sign envy. She also had some pretty good suspicions about the reasons for the disparity."

"Elizabeth assumed that because she had strong faith and trust, the Other Side didn't need to give her many signs, let alone, really big ones that were difficult to ignore. Being her Guide, I would have to admit that she was right. She lamented about this quite frequently. So, every once in a while I would feel guilty and toss her a little something. But I never went to the lengths you went to MacGregor."

"So, back to the health food store. During the course of their conversation, Vicky was engaging in her usual dismissal of all that was synchronistic, magical, awe-inspiring and other-worldly. Many of the occurrences they were speaking about pertained to a certain person who was currently in Vicky's life. It's unnecessary to get into the details of it. The important thing is that Elizabeth's frustration reached new heights. She proceeded to list off all the amazing things that have happened or that they've learned. Everything she stated was more than related, obvious and true, despite Vicky's unwillingness to accept them as such."

Awe rubs his hands together as his eyes glow with excitement. "Now we're getting to the good part. Knowing that you were Vicky's Guide and having repeatedly acknowledged your superior sign-sending abilities in the past, Elizabeth called out to you."

By the way, the reason Elizabeth knew about MacGregor is because Vicky has connected with him on multiple occasions while doing hypnosis and energy work.

Back to the story… "Right then and there, Elizabeth asked you to do something that Vicky could not dispute and that would also prove that everything she said to Vicky was right. Elizabeth also mentioned that she recognized that bagpipe music was probably not an option, but she was confident you could pull off something wonderful. And boy was she right!"

A super-sized grin spreads across both Awe and MacGregor's faces. "Not even seven minutes after Elizabeth made her request, Vicky's eyes and mouth registered shock and something else. 'What is it?' Elizabeth asked. Vicky muttered a stream of unintelligible words that included the phrase, 'wearing a kilt!' Elizabeth was naturally confused. She asked Vicky to repeat what she said and hoped this time she would get some coherent sentence out of her. Finally,

Vicky was able to convey that she had just seen a man pass by who was wearing a kilt."

"Now Elizabeth was annoyed. She thought her friend was just being obnoxious and making fun of her perceivably silly request. It took a while before Vicky convinced Elizabeth that she really saw something."

"At this point, Elizabeth, still incredulous, felt compelled to list off the many reasons why her friend was mistaken or crazy. 'This is a health food store. It's the middle of the week. There are no highland festivals currently going on at the time, nor is this a particularly Scottish area. There is absolutely no reason for someone to be a wearing a kilt, let alone in a health food store.' Of course, Vicky's response was 'I know, but it's what I saw.'"

"Determined to put an end to what she felt was a ridiculous discussion, Elizabeth arose from her seat and proceeded to search the store for some explanation."

"As you know, it didn't take long before she spotted with her very own eyes a man wearing a kilt, standing in line, waiting to pay the cashier for a beverage. Now, I wouldn't call it a traditional example, but it was a kilt, nonetheless. As expected,

Elizabeth returned to the table to let Vicky know she was right. Elizabeth's frustration and annoyance suddenly turned to excitement because she knew this was the sign she asked for."

"In the cockiest of tones, she declared, 'See, I'm right!' Elizabeth got what she wanted. And Vicky, though she tried, could not explain what she witnessed. She had no other option than to recognize and accept it as the sign it was. Vicky even went so far as to conclude out loud, 'so, all those other things are real, aren't they?' Unsurprisingly, Elizabeth rolled her eyes, and then uttered a single 'Duh!' in response."

"Invigorated by the victory of the moment, Elizabeth literally went on and on for days later about how brilliant you were and how grateful she was about your timing and execution. There was also another bonus for both your efforts. For a short time and to her relief, Elizabeth didn't have to listen to Vicky repeatedly question or dismiss things."

"So, to sum up this story…" Awe says while clapping. "Bravo, O Great MacGregor! Bravo!"

MacGregor stands up, takes a bow and proclaims with pride, "Yeah, that was a good day."

Awe gives MacGregor a high-five. "Damn straight!"

NEW DAY AND NEW REVELATIONS

Although she did not exhibit her usual enthusiasm, Evangeline nonetheless arrives at the office with a genuine smile on her face. *I will not be triggered in a negative way today*; she thinks to herself as she takes a seat at her desk.

Her message light is blinking. The first communication is from MacGregor who is requesting a status of their findings thus far. The second one is from Ellery who just called to say hello and tell her that he loved her. Evangeline's whole being felt warm and happy after hearing his voice and words.

Just as she is about to return MacGregor's call August approaches with some trepidation. Even though it wasn't his intention, he knows he upset her and feels really bad about it.

"Evangeline," he says with noticeable sadness and nervousness in his voice, "I'm sorry if I, um. I didn't mean to, well, you know. It's just that. I tried to, well. Anyway, I hope, um, that you are ok."

"It's alright August," she says, and she means it too.

August is so overcome with emotion; he instantly transforms into his Earthly looking self and draws Evangeline out of her seat and into his arms for a hug. She is truly moved by his gesture and just allows herself to be held. After what seems like an excessively long time passes, they finally break free from one another and just stand there looking into each other's eyes.

Evangeline then casts her gaze from his head all the way down to his toes and then back up again. "Damn August, you are so handsome!" she eventually declares while shaking her head and staring a little too hungrily for either's comfort. "Katia is going to have a really hard time focusing on the movies when she can look at all of that…"

August blushes. Evangeline hugs him roughly and plants a kiss on his exquisite cheek and then thanks him for being who he is. At that, he transforms back to his floating orb-like self and bids her farewell as he heads off to plow through the long queue of interviews that have yet to be completed.

Evangeline rings up MacGregor to fill him in on the latest developments. He answers abruptly and asks if he can call her right back. A few minutes later his gorgeous face pops up on her communication device's screen. "Sorry about that," he says, "I was on another line with my editor."

"Editor?" she asks.

"Yeah, he is finally getting back to us on our latest work."

"Work? Are you an author?"

"Yeah, I am. Awe and I have published a few books over the years. They are particular to guiding so you probably haven't heard of them. Our first one was volume 1 of our series 'A Guide's Guide to the Other Side'. It's called, 'Coming to the Other Side'. We then followed up with volume 2, 'On the Other Side'. Then there was volume 3, 'Leaving the Other Side, One Last Sip Before I Go'. After that, we released a companion guide called, 'A Guide's Guide to becoming a Guide'."

"Our latest work," he continues, "should be coming out by the year's end, assuming our editor and publisher can get it all together by then. It will be called, 'A Guide's Guide to Eating on the Other Side -

Eating through the Ages'. As you can imagine, this one is very close to our hearts."

"Impressive. I'll have to pick up some copies at Ye Olde Bookshop. Maybe you can even autograph them for me."

"I would be delighted. So enough about me, how are things progressing on your end?"

Evangeline proceeds to highlight some of the more important revelations from her department's investigation.

"Wow! This is turning out to be quite the mystery and much more complex than I would have ever imagined."

"More than any of us could have anticipated," she admits. "But we have everyone doing their utmost to bring this to resolution. We'll get there."

"Of course, you will. I can't help but wonder what it's going to mean when we do."

Evangeline forces a smile as an unsettling feeling starts to creep in. "Well. Let us just focus on pursuing the answers. Is there anything else?"

"No. I'm good. Take care Evangeline. And good luck."

Just as MacGregor's face fades out, O-bray-em's face comes into view. "O-bray-em, what a surprise!" she says.

O-bray-em looks like a kid who just found a stash of candy or toys. "I wanted to tell you as soon as I could. I found something!"

"Already?" Evangeline is so excited she could barely sit still in her chair.

"Yes. As you know, I have been in the healing business for a very long time. There are many therapeutic modalities and technologies that specialists like myself use to purge junk from souls who desire or require healing. Most of the negative aspects released are either neutralized or converted into something positive fairly immediately. There is, however, one exception. In more severe cases, a healing center may decide to perform what is called an 'emotional intervention' on their patient. The purpose of this type of procedure is to stabilize a soul and hopefully make them more receptive to and capable of addressing their issues."

He clears his throat, before continuing. "When someone undergoes an intervention, they are essentially having a big chunk of negative emotions extracted from them without having to understand or come to peace with said feelings. While it is preferable to have some intellectualization of these painful elements, it is sometimes necessary to forgo this nicety in extreme circumstances."

"Unlike other releasing mechanisms, the intervention process creates residual components that require lengthy and complicated disposal methods. Each healing facility who does this type of release must maintain an intermediary storage container on site to temporarily house their potent undesired discards. These collections are typically emptied out and sent to a main holding center on some regular basis depending upon their volume. Then about a couple of times during the year, the main facility will run a cleansing protocol, which will then eliminate the hazardous gunk out of existence."

"Here's the thing, the debris your team has identified inside the affected souls comes from one of these holding tanks."

"Are you sure?"

"Without a doubt. I've studied the output of these extractions many times. They have a signature or makeup that is rather unique. Somehow, that material infiltrated the Happy Juice and was ingested and thus became part of those who consumed it."

Evangeline's not-so-physical stomach starts to hurt. "Have you by any chance had an opportunity to examine the tainted Happy Juice as well?"

"I have. They contain larger quantities of the same debris in higher degrees of potency."

"I see. This main facility you speak of, where is it located?"

"Plane 6. For safety purposes, the distance as well as the small population made it an ideal spot to store the material."

"What about the intermediary containers?"

"As I've said, they are all on site in every healing facility that deals with more severe cases. All storage units should be properly secured and have measures to eliminate any potential for leakage. Inspections are done annually in an attempt to avoid any unpleasantries from occurring. The last one was done about six months ago."

"How many facilities would you say offer such a process and would thus have ugly leftovers from the process?"

"On the Other Side, there are a limited number of locations. Doc B's center, the Infirmary and the Crystal Power Group. There are also at least a dozen or so healing centers across multiple planes that are hooked up to the main facility, including mine of course."

"Is there a way of back tracking the debris to a particular location?"

"No."

"Is there any way of determining the source of the debris? The original souls who released them?"

"Unfortunately, no."

Evangeline rubs her temples and takes a long steady breath. "Is there something unusual about the debris that could help us better figure out where it came from?"

"Sorry," he says shaking his head.

"Alright. How easy is it to take a sample from these vats or whatever they are and inject their contents into another vat, say of Happy Juice?"

"Very easy. Each container has a sample port. Facilities typically do frequent drawings from the port to test concentration and other factors for both research and other purposes. The Happy Juice Distillery also uses sample ports to ensure quality and consistency of their output."

"Really? So, anyone could have done this at any time without anyone thinking twice about it."

"That's right." He hated to say it, but the truth sets us free. "I'm sorry Evangeline."

"It's alright. I appreciate your help here. Do you have any suggestions?"

"Aside from expanding your interview group, there is one thing you might be able to do to narrow things down. It's time consuming but I think it might be worthwhile."

"What is that?"

"Every healing center is required to log the additions made to their intermediary containers and keep track of how full they are at a given time." He shows her an example on her screen. "Someone from your team could backtrack this information and look for any quantity discrepancies. Mind you, these discrepancies will be small, because it doesn't take much of this stuff to cause issues. Unfortunately, this could all be a waste of time and effort, if the individual or individuals involved modified the documentation to cover their tracks."

"That makes sense. But just to be on the safe side, I will have a few of my team members do some cursory examinations. Of course, I will also update August with this information and have him expand his interviews to include employees of the healing centers as well as the Infirmary."

"Good idea. I will say Evangeline, if I were you, I would focus only on the facilities that are here on the Other Side. I can't see other dimension locations getting involved in Earth related matters and Happy Juice."

"I think you're right. It wouldn't be logical. By the way, do you have any theory as to why certain souls didn't have an adverse reaction?"

"I do. Souls with higher frequencies and little to no junk earn and acquire a protective mechanism when they attain a certain level. This protective aspect prevents any negativity of any kind from infiltrating any level of their already fairly clean selves. Without examining the souls in question, just from what I've been told, I have little doubt that the individuals who escaped unscathed, did so because they were protected."

"Wow! I never knew that. I cannot thank you enough and I don't know what we would have done without you."

"I'm sure your team would have gotten there sooner than you think. They are a fine group of souls with lots of experience and knowledge. Is there anything else I can do for you?"

"Nothing at this time. Again, thank you so much for coming here and helping. Will you be returning to your healing center and staying there for a while?"

"Yes. If you need something, just call."

"I will. Goodbye O-bray-em. Take care."

"You too." And with that, the screen goes blank.

Evangeline's mind is spinning from all the new information and added complexity that her department will need to deal with. She decides to pop in personally to each of her team's locations to update them with the latest, and unfortunately, add to the list of to-dos. Evangeline takes O-bray-em's advice by having her people only focus on Other Side facilities.

Upon their arrival at the Infirmary, Charles and Debra head straight to his boss' office. The door is already slightly ajar. Charles knocks and then peeks his head inside just enough to get Gordon's attention. "Is it alright for us to come in?" Charles asks.

Gordon smiles and then waves at them to enter. "Charles, Debra? What a surprise."

Debra smiles back. "Hello Gordon, it's nice to see you again. I'm just here for moral support."

Gordon's face shifts to confusion. "For what?"

Debra squeezes Charles' hand and encourages him to speak. Charles clears his throat nervously. "Well um, Gordon, you see, I'm here to… I have to um… I'll just say it. I am submitting my resignation to you. Of course, I can certainly stick around for a few more weeks to wrap things up and help transition everything. But after that, I am leaving the Infirmary for good."

His boss doesn't look as shocked as Debra would have anticipated. "Can I ask why? Not that I don't already have my suspicions. I know you have been troubled lately, but I guess I didn't know how much."

"I can't do it anymore," Charles declares simply. "I have lost my detachment and can't seem to shake off the tragedy of it all, even though souls eventually get better. I need to do something different. Something lighter, cheerier. I'm sorry."

"There is nothing for you to be sorry about," Gordon says. "I understand completely. This is not an easy place to work. And let's face it; you've been doing this a lot longer than most of us. You will be missed, but there is no reason for you to continue to stay in a place that makes you uncomfortable. Naturally, we would appreciate it if you could stay for a short time to help us changeover things. But honestly, if you think it's too much, you can leave as soon as you're ready."

Relief sweeps through Charles. He really didn't think it would be this easy. "Thank you, Gordon."

"No, Charles, thank you. Your dedication, compassion, and service over all these years have made a significant difference in so many souls' lives. We at the Infirmary will be forever grateful. I am just so sorry it's caused you so much despair as of late."

Charles starts to feel tears run down his not-truly-physical cheek. He's speechless. Debra speaks for him. "You are so kind Gordon. Thank you for making this difficult decision easier for Charles."

Debra and Charles each give Gordon a hug before leaving his office. "You alright?" Debra asks.

"Yeah, I'm ok. Thanks for being there."

"There is nowhere else I would rather be." She presses a kiss to his cheek. "Ok. I'm going to let you do what you need to do while I head back to the Science Archives to pull up a few items for my client Joseph. If you need me, I'm just a communication away."

"I'm fine. Thanks. See you at home later."

"Bye for now," she says before disappearing before his eyes.

Charles proceeds to make a list of all the things he needs and wants to do before he will be comfortable enough to leave. Surprisingly and with mixed feelings, his list is a lot shorter than he would have imagined.

DRAMA, MOTIVATION & SUSPECTS OH MY!

Ellery comes by to whisk Evangeline off for a quick bite at the Nostalgia café. "I really shouldn't," she says.

His face shows some disappointment. "Well if you don't think you can…"

Evangeline starts to change her mind. "Perhaps if we keep it short, maybe it won't be so…"

Hope fills Ellery's eyes.

"Let's do it," she announces with a big grin. "Besides, there are many reasons to celebrate. Lots of progress has been made. It would be good to get your opinion. So really, this is kind of like a working thing that just has some food. Yeah, that's it. Let's go, my love."

After Evangeline convinces both herself and Ellery that going to the Nostalgia is productive and logical, they both flash to one of the café's cozy red vinyl-looking booths. A waitress dressed entirely in pink approaches them shortly after their arrival to see if they are ready to order something.

Ellery and Evangeline both decide to have a mushroom swiss hamburger with grilled onions, lettuce, pickles and a touch of mayonnaise. They also ask their server to throw in two large sides of extra crispy fries and a chocolate milkshake for them to share. Ellery remembers to make a request for malt powder to be added to the cold creamy concoction for extra yumminess. After they complete their order, both of them say a silent thank you that there is no such thing as calories or risk of weight gain on the Other Side.

As they chow down on their perfectly prepared food and beverages, Evangeline updates Ellery on all the latest information they've uncovered since beginning the investigation. Ellery is impressed and amazed by how much they already know, along with the sheer complexity of it all. Evangeline can almost imagine wheels turning inside his head while he processes everything she just told him.

"I find it interesting," he begins, "how much happens here that we have no clue about. Who knew, the Other Side and other dimensions collect emotional waste, let alone that the stuff sticks around long enough to be potentially harmful to someone. That's crazy."

"I know. I was floored by this revelation."

"I totally agree with O-bray-em. There is no reason anyone outside the Other Side would have any cause to interfere with Earthly incarnations and Happy Juice. So, my money is on one of our three facilities."

"Which one?"

Ellery looks upward as if the solution to their quandary is stuck to the ceiling. "Good question. I think the interviews are going to be critical in determining that answer. I will also have to say, I highly doubt your examiners are going to find any discrepancy in the logs. Anyone who can pull off something this elaborate and complex without someone noticing is not stupid. There is no way whoever did this, failed to modify the logs to cover their tracks. Solving this thing is going to come down to profiling each employee at each facility to find the soul who has the greatest motivation."

"So, you are certain that our culprit works at one of the healing facilities?"

He shakes his head. "No, but I think it's the most likely place to look given that each of these locations have access to the substance in question. That's not to say that it couldn't be someone from somewhere else who was aware of what these facilities had in storage. But they would also have to have technical knowledge of how to extract and then inject the substances into the Happy Juice. Not to mention, they would also need access to both the Distillery and intermediary holding tanks without anyone thinking twice about it."

Evangeline ponders Ellery's points carefully. "True. But what you haven't mentioned is the possibility that more than one soul is involved. Someone who has access to Happy Juice tanks and someone who is familiar with the emotional leftovers housed in the healing facilities."

"Good point. That would certainly make pulling off this plan a lot easier."

"Unfortunately, no one is standing out as a potential suspect. At least not yet. August's team just needs to continue plowing through the list until something shouts out at them."

"Everything is coming together," Ellery reassures. "It's just going to take a little more time. I will say you were darn lucky to have tracked down O-bray-em so quickly."

"I know. His reputation is certainly warranted. He is the man! Did you know they have a section dedicated to him at the Archives?"

"Wow! No, I didn't. That's really different."

"It is. It now makes me wonder if they have special sections dedicated to other individuals."

"You'll have to ask Viola."

"Yeah, I will. I will have to say though, she kind of made me feel like I was stupid that I never heard of O-bray-em before."

"Oh Evangeline, I wouldn't take it personally," he says. "Perhaps she's so enamored by the guy she can't imagine anyone not knowing what she knows and feeling the same way. Keep in mind though, she's literally surrounded every day by data of all types, so she can be a resource to help others find the information they require. It's easy to lose track of the fact that other souls are not in constant proximity to and thus may be unfamiliar with such a wealth of knowledge."

"You are right," she says. "Thanks, my love. By the way, is there anything on your end to report?"

"Nope. Just continuing to do testing. Haven't come up with my own spark of inspiration yet. Although, after all this Other Side intrigue, perhaps I might develop something applicable to our own dimension's challenges."

"Hmm. Interesting idea. Oh, I meant to ask you about your milkshake with the added malt. Did it restore your faith in the frosty beverage?"

Ellery grins ear to ear, proudly displaying the chocolatey mustache above his lips. "Yes indeed."

"Glad to hear it. You know, I just had a thought. Given that it's one of the facilities in question, do you think it would be a good idea… I mean, would it be appropriate if I contacted your friend's sweetheart about all this? The one who works at the Infirmary."

"Actually Evangeline, I don't think that would be wise. You want to keep personal relationships out of this. Just let your team do what they do best. It will all flesh itself out in the end."

"That makes sense. Thanks. Well, I would love to linger here, but I do need to go back to check on things. See you later."

"Ta Ta for now!"

Within an instant, both of them are back at their respective work sites.

August decides that he is relieved that he doesn't have any eyes, because he knows they would be bloodshot and crossing at this point. He also suspects he would be banging his head against a wall if he had one. With too many of them to count, he has lost track of the number of interviews he's conducted so far. There are still many more for him to get through.

All the questions and answers are running together in his mind in a jumbled mess. Although August doesn't typically feel tired or overwhelmed, the sheer volume of what needs to be done and kept track of is starting to take a toll.

To help him reclaim the clarity, strength and focus he will need for the next interview, August drifts into a void space. This energetic neutral zone, if you will, allows one to achieve a state of bliss in total silence, stillness and nothingness. It gives a soul the ability to just be and thus restore a sense of balance and peace. With balance, all good things are possible.

Keep in mind, there are seemingly endless options for the inhabitants of the Other Side to find peace, comfort, clarity and virtually any other positive aspect they desire at a given moment. While some may opt to utilize physical aspects like places or food items, others employ less tangible mechanisms like voids or energetic healing technology to get the same effect. Again, everything on the Other Side is about choice.

As August enters the void, he feels an immediate shift. It's like being washed clean, then shined, and given a wonderful hug afterward. Love pours into and radiates from every level of his being, as does peace. His mind effortlessly clears and relishes in the stillness. Everything feels easy and doable. Every level of his being is smiling from pure infinite joy.

As much as August would like to linger in the wonderfulness of the void, he knows he needs to get back to work. So, despite some hesitation, he returns to the interview facility to join the rest of his team.

Back at his desk now, he ushers in the next soul on his list.

Happy Juice Distillery manager, Eleanor takes a seat across from where he hovers. This woman is clearly a no-nonsense gal with little interest in fashion or frivolity. Her dark brown hair is pulled back tightly into a bun just above her neckline with only a couple of pins to secure it. She's dressed in a plain white shirt, brown slacks and a matching brown jacket. On her feet are practical non-descript flat brown shoes. There are no shiny buttons, bows, clips, jewelry or adornment of any kind on her person. The facial expression she wears is so unreadable; August imagines that she would make an excellent poker player.

"I've never been one to gamble," she says plainly.

August makes an adjustment to his thought filter to ensure that she only hears what he wants her to hear. "It's not for everyone," he says. "Anyway, thank you Eleanor for agreeing to this interview."

Now Miss Neutral is laughing. "Agree is not exactly what I would call it." Her arms cross tightly over her chest as she says it.

"Do you have some issue with us conducting an investigation?"

"No, I understand why you need to look into things, but I have to say I am not sure what my people have to do with all of this," Eleanor states way too defensively for August's comfort. If he had an eyebrow it would certainly be raised at this point.

"We have souls who have experienced adverse responses to a tainted version of Happy Juice. Not only does your facility produce Happy Juice, but as per our testing, the results show some of your tanks contain contaminated versions of Happy Juice. Why wouldn't we question the employees who work at your clearly compromised facility?"

Eleanor shifts uncomfortably in her seat as a stray hair escapes from her perfectly constrained hairdo. "Well, granted these are certainly undesired developments, but I cannot imagine any of my workers being responsible for such a thing."

"Are you saying things can go on in your facility that none of you would have any knowledge of or involvement in?"

"Um, I, well. It's just that. Let's just say, it's not out of the realm of possibility for something to happen without someone noticing. I mean we're not locked down or overrun with security. This is the Other Side. Hello!"

"This may be the Other Side, but souls are souls. And not every soul has the best intentions or even the capabilities to do what is best all the time."

"True."

"Listen Eleanor, just like you, I have a job to do. Part of my job is to ask questions, whether you think they're warranted or not. I need for you and your people to help me, to help all of us. This is not a judgment of how you are running the Distillery. This is not a condemnation of the character of your employees. This is just an investigation. We just need to find the truth, so this can be over."

Eleanor shifts her position in her seat and nods in understanding. "I'm sorry. You're right. Ask me whatever you like."

August runs through a bunch of questions. Nothing appears to raise any flags or concern until he asks about recent changes in the facility or staffing.

"We did have someone leave us a short while ago," Eleanor says with noticeable uneasiness.

"Why is that?"

"Well, it's kind of complicated."

"Ok. Just tell me as best as you can."

Eleanor nervously fidgets and taps her fingers against the top of the desk. "Tom, that's his name, he was with the Distillery for I don't know, at least a decade. He was generally cheerful, super social and really easy to be around. Anyway, one day, a few months back, he comes into work clearly agitated. A few of his co-workers asked him if he was ok, at which he responded with a loud 'no!' and a pretty severe grimace on his face."

"Naturally, everyone tried to comfort him and ask him about what was wrong. After a bit of coaxing, he finally explained. He told the team that his soul mate

Helen recently returned from Earth and was currently undergoing treatment in the Infirmary."

Eleanor's neutral expression softens with sadness. "Apparently, she had a very tough go of it and was so traumatized she couldn't make her normal transition to the Other Side. When he went to visit her, she didn't even recognize him and she was so upset, they had to remove him from the room so they could get her to calm down. It was ugly and heartbreaking, and he was pissed."

"He then told everyone that he felt responsible for her suffering. Tom said it was because he produced the substance that ultimately caused her to agree to experience the horror that broke her. After that, he submitted his resignation and said he could no longer be part of something that prevents people from seeing the truth of what they are signing up for. 'The game is rigged' he said. 'People should go in with eyes wide open or avoid the wretched place altogether.' And then he left. We haven't heard from him since."

August tries not to sound too snarky, but it was difficult. "Well gee Eleanor, if that's not a strong motive to sabotage Happy Juice, I don't know what is."

"I guess if you think about it and put it that way, perhaps it warrants further inquiry."

"It absolutely does," he says. "So, where can I find Tom?"

"I suppose he's either at home or waiting somewhere in Infirmary C."

"If you can give me his last known coordinates that would be helpful."

"I will have my assistant send them to you." Her gaze lowers slightly before she adds, "I'm sorry August. I guess I was blinded by pride and foolishness."

"I appreciate you saying that."

"If Tom is responsible for all of this, it would pain me deeply, but the truth must be known. I would ask one thing of you though. Please be gentle with him. He's been through a lot. If he did do this, it was coming from a place of hurt, not mal intent."

"I know that Eleanor. And rest assured we will proceed with utmost compassion."

"Thank you."

"Thank you."

After Eleanor leaves, August makes some final additions to his notes. He then goes to find

Evangeline so he could tell her about what he just discovered.

The sand is soft as silk and white as snow. Turquoise blue water, lightly capped in white, laps up gently to the shore and retreats just as gently over and over again in soothing rhythm. Lush green palms stand majestically like sentries watching each end of the strip of beach. The delicate breeze that flows through the air carries with it the scent of Earthly tropical flowers, salt and suntan oil. Two rows of highly cushioned chairs sit partially sunken into the sand, eagerly awaiting someone to sit in them. The only sounds that can be heard are that of rolling waves.

The beautiful and serene beach sits on a secluded island lovingly called the Isle of Aaah.

Aaah is the creation of MacGregor and Awe. It was designed as a place of peace and respite for Guides and Guardians who sometimes need to get away.

The island offers calm, beauty and quiet to all who come there, so they can think or just be for a while. Daily frustrations and sadness slip away the moment someone steps onto the sand. The water and the breeze work effortlessly and instantly to carry away negativity and restore a sense of balance and hope. Delicious food and beverages flow freely to satisfy cravings and offer further comfort.

A great uneasiness has settled into MacGregor and Awe's beings. Desperate for some escape and to re-stabilize themselves, they head to their island. The Guides kick off their flip flops and plop down onto their respective lounge chairs. Both of them manifest side tables, each of which holds a large tropical drink adorned with colorful fruit, a paper umbrella and a long sturdy straw.

Awe takes the first sip. "Oh yes, that is wonderful," he says as the cool liquid flows down his not-truly-physical throat.

MacGregor follows suit and lets out a long satisfying sigh. "This is the life."

"Uh, huh."

"Do you want to set up a fire?" MacGregor asks.

"Sure. But if we do, we'll need to roast some marshmallows and make s'mores."

"Of course."

Within a flash, a circle of stone with a pile of wood in its center appears on the sand, far enough away that the water can't reach it. A moment later a crackling fire glows warm and bright within the circle.

Awe and MacGregor stand eagerly with long sticks in hand with marshmallows stuck on the ends. Each moves their cloud-like blob toward the fire to brown. It doesn't take but a moment before they are stuffing the gooey sweet, charred magic into sandwiches of graham cracker and dark chocolate. No milk chocolate for them.

MacGregor takes the first bite. "This is glorious," he announces as his mouth and chin become covered in sticky sweetness and crumbs.

Awe simply groans and then carefully licks each finger to ensure that he gets every drop. Afterward, he takes a hearty gulp of his frozen fruity concoction. Before he knows it, he's gritting his teeth and holding his head, as pain shoots through it.

"Brain freeze huh?" MacGregor asks with both sympathy and amusement in his voice.

"Ugh, yes."

"That's what happens when you drink something cold too fast and choose to hang around the Other Side in a physical form."

"Yeah, yeah, yeah."

The boys sit in silence for a while just watching the water and taking in the peace and beauty of Aaah. While they do, they feel their entire beings coming back into perfect balance. After some time passes, Awe and MacGregor are joined by a fellow Guide named Harry.

Harry is quite the character and likes to wear Earthly swimming fashions from a variety of eras every time he steps onto the island. This time, he is sporting something from the 1920's that covers a good deal of his body with blue and white stripes. His head is adorned with a straw hat with a matching blue band above its brim. And just to complete the picture, he is donning an unnaturally oversized mustache above his lip. Harry stands in front of MacGregor and Awe striking a pose with fists held high and muscles bulging from his tanned arms.

MacGregor and Awe can't help but smile. "Brilliant!" Awe says.

"The mustache is a very nice touch," MacGregor remarks while nodding.

"I know, right! These shorts are super loose though." Harry frowns. "No support for the jewels."

Awe and MacGregor nod with serious looks on their faces. "Definitely need support for the jewels," they both say simultaneously.

Harry takes a seat. "I thought I might find you guys here. I just got back from the convention and heard about all the drama and intrigue. Craaay-zeeee stuff. Oh, and poor Elliot. I just can't believe it."

"I know," MacGregor says. "It's very disconcerting. So, how was the convention?"

Harry covers his mouth, fakes a yawn, and then proceeds to make loud snoring sounds. "Booor-ing. Well except for what happened at the Larry O show, that is."

This gets Awe and MacGregor's attention. "What happened?" Awe asks.

"First of all, you should know that I did not listen to the guy speak, nor did I have any intention to do so. So, all my information is nothing more than hearsay."

"Fine. No one here is holding you to anything. Just tells us," MacGregor urges impatiently.

"About midway through Larry O's speech, the door swings open and this Guide name Paulette bursts into the room and starts screaming at the top of her lungs."

"Holy moley capoley!" MacGregor says as his eyes go wide.

"Yup, that pretty much says it. Anyway, Paulette called Larry O a 'lazy, sadistic moron' and then went on to say the following:"

Harry makes quotes in the air with his fingers before continuing. "Isn't it bad enough that we trick people into going to a place where they will ultimately suffer and usually fail at what they're trying to accomplish? We shouldn't even be sending anyone to Earth anymore. It's ugly and it's a game no one can win. But then a low vibrational piece of doo doo like yourself comes along to make things worse. You have the utter gall to suggest that Guides don't even try to help but just sit back and watch. What is wrong with you? And what is wrong with all of you? How can you sit here listening to such idiocy? You should all be ashamed of yourselves. I know I am feeling ashamed to be a Guide right now."

"Wow!"

"I know. But wait, there's more. Then Paulette decides that expressing is not enough. She suddenly runs toward the podium and then starts punching Larry O as hard as she can over and over. He must have been in a state of shock because he just stands there and lets her hit him. Some of the Guides from the audience had to run up on stage and pull her off him. It was like Jerry Springer on the Other Side."

MacGregor and Awe are speechless, which says a lot. All they can do is shake their heads and stare at their friend's face hoping that he will break into a smile and say something like, "gotcha, only kidding!" But Harry was dead serious, and he wasn't inclined to smile anytime soon.

Awe rubs at his temples. "I hesitate to ask, but what happened next?"

Harry explains, "The conference ended abruptly as one would expect. Battered and embarrassed, Larry O disappeared as fast as he could. I don't think we'll be hearing about the 'Just Watch' movement or whatever they call it again. As for Paulette, she eventually calmed down and allegedly left to tender her resignation as a Guide and then hide out in her country home for a while. Everyone returned to discover that Contracts are on hold and Happy Juice ain't so happy. So here I am."

MacGregor turns to Awe. "We should tell Evangeline and August about this."

"I think you're right."

Harry looks somewhat confused. "I don't understand. What does the Larry O fiasco have to do with the Happy Juice situation?"

"Dude, Paulette has motive."

"Just because she's disillusioned and disgruntled, it doesn't mean she sabotaged the Happy Juice. Let's face it, most Guides get discouraged with the whole process at some time or another. I mean, that's why therapy is required. It helps us make sure we stay ok. Of course, every once in a while, the burden becomes too great and someone needs to quit. But that doesn't mean anyone is going to do something drastic to put a wrench in the process before they leave."

Awe thinks back to the heated discussion that ensued at the last therapy meeting and feels a chill run through him. If he were honest with himself, he would have to admit that Joanne could be a suspect too.

"Everything you said is true," he finally says. "However, something unusual has happened. We must consider all scenarios to resolve this thing. And while I do not want to think that a fellow Guide is responsible for this, I cannot exclude the possibility. The convention incident stands out as something Evangeline's team might want to look into. And MacGregor, we might also want to mention what was said at group therapy, especially by Joanne."

MacGregor begrudgingly concurs.

Harry nods in agreement. "Would you like me to come with you guys?"

"That would be helpful Harry, thanks." MacGregor looks out onto the water making a mental request for calm. "We don't have to rush there now," he says. "Why don't we, you know, just be for a while?" Unsurprisingly, everyone agrees.

Harry is relieved that he can linger for a little longer. Before he settles down into a lounge chair, he conjures up a frozen drink in one hand and a warm gooey s'more in the other. Awe cautions him not to drink too swiftly. Harry is fully aware of the risk of brain freeze and sips at his tropical fruit concoction very slowly, savoring every drop.

The three friends sit quietly for a while until a deep feeling of peace settles back into them. Although none of them want to leave, they know they must. And so, with a flash, all three Guides are now standing by the edge of Evangeline's desk. She surveys their odd attire curiously and dusts away sand from the top of her desk. "Gentleman, how can I help you?"

Just as MacGregor is about to speak, August suddenly appears beside them hovering excitedly through the air. "Evangeline," he says impatiently, "boy oh boy, have I got something to tell you."

"You'll have to wait your turn August. MacGregor and Awe got here first."

NARROWING THINGS DOWN

Evangeline can hardly believe what she just heard. As if the current situation isn't dramatic enough, they now have more craziness to plow through. "Guides punching Guides and having screaming matches. If I didn't know any better, I would think I was on some playground with a bunch of eight-year-olds on Earth instead of on the Other Side."

All of them agree these are strange times. August acknowledges that Paulette is definitely someone to add to the list, but says he thinks he has an even more compelling suspect. His claim evokes both surprise and curiosity in everyone. After he tells them the whole story about Tom, the group is noticeably quiet and emotional. "I know," he says, "sad stuff. But it all fits. Motive, means and even opportunity."

Evangeline wipes away some tears from her eyes. "I think you're right," she says. "But August, we need to proceed with great delicacy and compassion. We are not dealing with a maniacal troublemaker. This is someone who is justifiably grieving and angry."

"Of course. How do you want to do this?"

Evangeline thinks for a moment before speaking. "Our choice of location is important. I think the more neutral and peaceful, the better. I'd like to call in an Angel and maybe a close associate of Tom's. Perhaps his previous Guide, um, maybe a therapist from the Mind Matters Healing Institute as well."

"With respect," Awe interjects, "having too many souls there at a time might make him feel ganged up on."

"Yes, I see your point. I just want resources available to make this as easy as I can."

"If it were me," Harry says, "I would just have an Angel present. But if things should get out of control, have the therapist and former Guide waiting on standby."

"Good idea," August says.

"What about the location?"

All three Guides simultaneously proclaim out loud, "Aaah!"

August and Evangeline are clearly confused. August decides to ask the critical question. "Are you all having some parallel epiphany, out of body experience or what?"

MacGregor laughs. "Nothing like that. Awe and I have this island we created a while back. We call it the Isle of Aaah. It's peaceful, healing, calming, quiet and beautiful. It would be a perfect place to do what you need to do."

"We also have stellar food and beverage options available," Awe adds proudly.

Harry nods and smiles. "I recommend the frozen tropical drinks and s'mores. If you're also looking for something savory to have with them, the guacamole and chips pair well."

Awe's stomach grumbles at the mere mention. "Yeah, good stuff. But don't drink too fast. You don't want brain freeze."

"Yes, well, food and beverages aside, this island of yours sounds like a good plan."

MacGregor jots down the coordinates and hands them to Evangeline.

"Thank you," she says. "All of you have been truly helpful."

After the trio leaves, August and Evangeline make plans. "I'll pop out to the island to check things out and then track down Tom's current location," he says.

"And I'll connect with the Angel Council and request their assistance."

"It's a deal. Catch you later," August says before leaving.

The Angel Council resides in a much higher realm than the Other Side, as do the Angels they represent. Angels are primarily messengers and protectors, who also offer healing, comfort, wisdom and sometimes serve more administrative objectives. Some Angels fulfill duties that have bearing on all of the universe and heaven, while others support only a subset. For instance, there are Angels whose sole purpose and assignments are specifically tied to Earth.

Human beings primarily interface with Guardian type Angels and may sometimes encounter more powerful Archangels such as Michael, Gabriel, Raphael and Uriel. Keep in mind, while Angels often visit Earth, they will never incarnate onto Earth. And although they can intervene when someone is in danger, there is a limit to how much they can involve themselves in the lives of Earth's inhabitants.

Evangeline punches in the coordinates for the Angel Council on her communication device. A beautiful and luminescent face appears on her display as soothing music plays suddenly within her head. "Evangeline," a soft, strangely calming voice says, "how lovely to hear from you. What can we do for you today?"

"Melodia, I need your help on a sensitive matter."

"Of course. Tell me what's going on."

Evangeline provides a synopsis of the situation as best as she can and asks Melodia what she might recommend particularly as it applies to dealing with Tom. The Angel Council Leader concurs that Angelic presence would be helpful. "And I know the perfect Angel to send you," she says.

"I'm very grateful. Who are you sending us and when can I expect them to arrive here?"

Melodia smiles as light and love pours into Evangeline. Boy oh boy does she love Angels.

"Serena will be arriving tomorrow. She is finishing up an assignment and won't be available till then. But dearest Evangeline, she is definitely worth the wait. You could check with Annabelle on this, Serena's name means calm, clarity, tranquility, peace or serenity. And that is exactly what everyone in her midst will feel. It will be difficult for anyone to become agitated or upset in her company. Even the orneriest of folks can't help but smile around her."

"She sounds perfect." Evangeline then provides the Angel Leader with the coordinates and thanks her.

"You are most welcome. Good luck and take care."

After Evangeline disconnects from her communication with Melodia, O-bray-em pops up onto her screen. "Do you have a minute?" he asks, near bursting with excitement.

"I do. What is it?"

"I was thinking about those poor souls who are still suffering from the residual effects of consuming tainted Happy Juice. I felt compelled to come up with a solution that could alleviate, if not eliminate all adverse manifestations."

"That would be extremely helpful," Evangeline says as she thinks about the possibility.

"Happily," he continues, "I've done just that. I have been able to construct a new algorithm and recalibrate one of our releasing devices to selectively target specific emotional debris for removal. It enables us to pull out only those items that were introduced to the affected souls by the compromised Happy Juice and leave all other emotional baggage untouched. This means that all patients who go through this process will experience full healing and restoration to levels prior to ingesting the contaminated substance."

"That's amazing!" Evangeline proclaims with a deep feeling of relief flowing through her.

"The only thing is," he adds, "I would need them to come to my healing center."

"That's not an issue. I will have a few of my team members round them up and bring them to you. When would you like them to come there? Should they show up at a specific coordinate within your facility?"

O-bray-em provides Evangeline with the desired location information and sets up a time for the next day. "My own team," he explains, "will require some preparation prior to your team's arrival, so tomorrow is perfect."

"How long will all of this take?" she asks.

"Not long at all. This process is very efficient and fast. Unless something unusual presents itself, everyone should be back on the Other Side by the next day."

"Wow! That's incredible. I have to say, your reputation is certainly warranted."

O-bray-em blushes at her remark. "Um well, thanks."

"No. Thank you! If you need anything else just let us know. My people will be there tomorrow as requested."

After the display goes dark to signal the end of their communication, Evangeline makes the rounds to alert all of her team members of the latest developments. She arranges for a few Guides, along with two of her Problem-Solving team members to escort the affected souls to Jaylon for treatment. Tom has already been tracked down and is scheduled to be interviewed on the Isle of Aaah.

Everything is falling into place, she thinks. The end of this ordeal seems to be close at hand.

Meanwhile, having already set up things for Tom, August decides to make a little visit to Paulette. Her country home, as they called it, looks like something out of an old Earthly western. Endless lush green fields, majestic horses running wildly, a bright red barn with a couple of happy black and white cows grazing in a nearby pasture all greet him upon his arrival.

He passes through a gated entrance and takes a long, twisting dirt road, lined with rustic wood fencing up to a wide, all wood ranch house. At its center are tall intricately carved double wooden doors with wrought iron handles that look more like twisted rope. A pair of tan, well-used boots is parked next to the door along with an empty bucket. A few feet over are two rocking chairs and a small table on which a jar of daisies sit cheerfully.

August manifests a loud knock and then calls out to Paulette. The doors edge open. A fresh-faced, golden-haired beauty wearing blue jeans and a plaid western shirt emerges. The loops of her denim pants are threaded with a simple brown belt. At its center is a huge silver buckle with the same twisted rope symbol that decorates her door. She smiles. "Yes, how can I help you?"

"My name is August," he says. "I work with the Problem-Solving department and am currently helping in an ongoing investigation. Could I ask you a few questions?"

"I don't see why not. Please come in," she says as she waves him inside.

The interior of her home could be best described as a deluxe log cabin complete with high beams and a copious amount of wood on every wall. The décor is a comfortable western chic that features a neutral color scheme of earth tones and black. Above the roughhewn wooden mantel of her fireplace is a magnificent painting, framed by two, horseshoe-shaped sconces on each side. The picture of cowboys riding on horses looks so real, August could swear he smells the scent of worn leather, sweat, grass and even manure in the air.

"Nice place," he says.

"Thanks. I like it."

"Any reason for the western theme?"

"One of my most favorite memories on Earth was when I visited my Aunt and Uncle's ranch in Montana. The land and the horses always made me feel happy and peaceful. So, when I got to the Other Side and they said I could live anywhere I wanted, this is the first thing that came to mind. But I know you are not here to talk to me about my home décor."

"No, I'm not. Are you aware of the Happy Juice situation that arose while you were attending the Guide convention?" he asks.

Paulette does not hesitate to say that she is. But before he could respond, August becomes temporarily distracted by the sight of a magnificent guitar leaning up against the couch upon which she now sits.

"Do you play?" he asks.

"Yes. I have for years. I was actually in a small band on Earth at one time. It comforts me to play."

"I used to play," he admits, feeling surprisingly sentimental as he says it. "At one time, I considered running off with my buddies and forming a band, but I was too practical and just let the dream slip away. Every now and then I think about what could have been."

"Were you any good?"

"They said I was. The only thing I do know is that I enjoyed it very much."

"You should try playing again," she says with a contagious grin.

"I might. That guitar you have over there is pretty nice."

"Thanks. It's an exact replica of the one I had on Earth. My Dad gave it to me. Despite him preferring that I pick something more stable or practical, he was super supportive of me following my dream. One day he just surprised me with it. He told me, 'you never know unless you try.' He didn't want me to always wonder what if, or be plagued by wouldas, couldas and shouldas like he was."

"Did he ever go to see you play in public?"

"He did. And he told me I was a natural and that I should give it all I got. And I did. While I didn't make a million bucks, I lived pretty well and more importantly, I loved what I did."

"That's great Paulette. I'm happy for you. Anyway, we should probably get back to the important subject at hand. What did you think when you heard about what happened when you were gone?"

"Honestly, I laughed."

This was not the response he was expecting. "You thought it was funny that a bunch of souls were overcome with terror, rage, despair and other not-so-pleasant emotions?"

"Well no, not that." Her eyes suddenly fill with sadness. "I'm not a monster. I don't want anyone to suffer. I've worked as a Guide for at least twenty-five years and have done everything I could possibly think of to help souls avoid suffering."

"But?"

"But it's not easy. The game, as they often call it, is kind of rigged. And getting through to people on Earth is a monumental task that takes a toll. Happy Juice is an absurd part of the process that helps us trick souls into agreeing to something totally unappealing and difficult at best. I guess at first, I thought it was humorous that someone decided to make a mockery of it. Of course, the result is not funny at all. It's terrible."

"Feeling as you do, would you ever consider doing something to force a change in the situation?"

"Are you suggesting that I had anything to do with this?"

"I might. After all, you said a lot of things at the convention that indicated you have more than a little anger and disillusionment about the whole going to Earth thing."

Paulette nods. "I see. This is all about the Larry O fiasco. Did I lose my temper? Sure. Did I punch the idiot? Without a doubt and quite frankly I would do it again. And am I considering a job change? You bet! But did I sabotage Happy Juice to cause suffering just to make some stupid point? No way! You, my dear August, are sniffing at the wrong boots."

August studies Paulette's eyes, body language and voice for any discrepancies with what she just stated. Nothing is shooting off any alarms in him. His "spidey sense" as he likes to call it, tells him she is speaking the truth. As a matter of fact, the minute he met her, he knew she wasn't responsible. But he needed to ask the questions anyway.

"I believe you," he says without any hesitation.

"Well thanks I guess."

"So, if you didn't do this, do you have any idea who might have gone to such extreme lengths to make a point as you so eloquently put it?"

"Not really. Truth be told, I think there are way too many souls out there who have the motive to do something like this."

"Really? You think this is a long standing and widespread issue that's somehow reached a tipping point?"

"I do. I think it's why someone like Larry O came up with such a bonehead idea as he did. He can't say what's really bothering him and yet feels responsible to stay on in some capacity even if it's useless. Larry O can't articulate the true struggle he's having."

August can't help but be impressed. "Hmm, interesting. Well if you feel that way, why did you attack him instead of helping him work through his feelings?"

"I was in the heat of the moment at the convention. And let's be clear, this revelation, if you can call it that, it just came to me now."

"I think your instincts have some merit. Quite frankly, until you said it, I agreed with you about him being a lazy, sadistic moron."

At August's admission, Paulette smiles widely. "You are a smart man."

"I've been told that. But I think you are a smart woman."

"I've been told that."

"Well, I've taken up enough of your time, so…" August says.

"It was nice meeting you August. Let me know if you want to play sometime."

"Thanks, I will. Take care and good luck." And with that, August disappears from Paulette's not-so-humble abode and reappears in front of Evangeline's desk.

Evangeline is radiating a peace that August can't put his finger on. "Are you um having a moment there?" he asks.

"Mmmm. I am."

"And what brought all of this on?"

"Well besides having things finally fall into place, I received a big surge of love, light and peace from Melodia."

"Ah, I see. Angel healing energy is the bomb! I have to say, I'm really looking forward to being in an Angel's presence tomorrow. I can use a little somethin' somethin'."

"No doubt," Evangeline says smiling. "I pray that Serena, that's the Angel's name, is able to help Tom so we can get to the truth and put this thing to rest once and for all."

"I second that. By the way, I had a little visit with Paulette."

"You did? What did you find out?"

"She's not our gal," he states without hesitation before filling her in on their conversation.

"Her observations are both interesting and disturbing," Evangeline remarks.

"They are. But these are strange times. If we are going to solve this, we need to be totally honest with ourselves, even if we don't like it."

"I agree. When you tracked down Tom, how did he appear to you?"

"I only viewed him from a distance. We never spoke. I had Lydia set up an appointment with him. She said he seemed ok."

"What did she say to him?"

"She told him there is an investigation going on regarding Happy Juice and that all past and present employees of the Distillery are being requested to participate in an interview. Lydia said he kind of shrugged it off and said he didn't know what he could tell us, but he would be alright with us asking him a few questions."

"That's good. I guess I'm kind of surprised he didn't appear nervous or agitated about the topic."

"It's not like he was jumpin' for joy about it, but no, he didn't get upset or anything. She did say he seemed preoccupied though. Of course, he was waiting to see Helen at the time, so that's understandable. He's also had some time to calm down since quitting his job at the Distillery, so that could account for more control."

"Do you think he's still our guy?"

"Good question. He certainly appears to be our most likely option from what we've identified thus far."

"I know. Everything lines up with him. Motive, means and opportunity as you stated before. No one looks better for this than Tom."

"We'll see what happens. I just hope I don't trigger some meltdown in the guy or break him any more than he already is."

"Nor do I. But I feel pretty confident that we have everything in place to avoid a catastrophe."

"I think you're right. By the way, that island is amazing. The minute you step onto it, it's like total bliss and peace. It's great. Honestly, I'm sorely tempted to show up tomorrow with a physical form so I can indulge in all the treaties and beverages the place offers. Having the whole package is intriguing to me."

"That's up to you," Evangeline says as her mind drifts briefly back to the awe-inspiring sight of August dancing in their office.

"Yeah, I got me some moves and a body to match!" he says.

"August!"

"Evangeline!"

"Very well, see you tomorrow. Have a good evening."

"You too."

Before he disappears, Evangeline could swear she hears Latin music playing in the background. *Damn, he's good*, she thinks.

14

AN ANGEL STEPS ONTO A BEACH

Hawaiian music plays softly in the background. The sand has been whitened and polished to perfection to create a lovely contrast to the deep, blue-green water that surrounds it. The wave pattern flowing in and out of shore is set to a rhythm which promotes optimal relaxation.

A long wooden picnic table is adorned with flowers and a delicious array of foods and beverages that will remain at their peak regardless of how much time passes. Brightly colored cushions sit atop the wooden benches that frame each side of the table, providing both comfort and style for all who come there.

A large sandcastle, complete with a moat sits off to the side as does a pile of aquatic items that guests can enjoy. Buckets, sand molds, shovels and even cheerful blow-up floats await those who wish to play on the island. For more serious entertainment, a dock stretches out from one end of the beach. Tied to it are four jet skis and a large motorboat.

The very manly MacGregor stands beside Awe with hands on hips wearing a grass skirt over his shorts and a crown of flowers on top of his head. Awe decided to go for something more subtle and stick with his usual Hawaiian shirt with shorts and flip flops. Both assess the results of their efforts and smile.

"It looks good."

"It does," MacGregor says before adjusting the background music and then swirling in place with arms stretched wide.

Awe looks at his friend Guide curiously, not sure what to expect. Before he knows it, MacGregor starts to shake and gyrate his hips along to the music. He then proceeds to perform a full hula routine, complete with hand gestures that tell a riveting tale of love and loss.

After his almost soothing story-telling dance ends, he transitions to a swifter and far more risky routine. He raises his hands in the air and makes some loud noise to add to the drama he is trying to create. A long-handled fiery object suddenly appears in each of them.

He cues the drums to accompany him as he performs a traditional and rather dangerous Polynesian fire dance. His arm movements are exceptionally fast and create the most hypnotic of sights including large circles of glowing flames. It's like extreme baton twirling with the added risk of being burnt or cut.

Until the mid-twentieth century these types of dances were traditionally done with long machete-like knives. No fire was involved. A Samoan dancer named Freddie Letuli changed all of that in 1946.

Henceforth, knives were wrapped in towel-like material and soaked in alcohol and then lit for the dance. The effect was dramatic and well received. As is the effect MacGregor is orchestrating on the beach at this very moment. Thankfully, the Other Side ensures he will never come to any harm by engaging in such behavior.

Awe is simply awestruck by what he witnesses. *Fire and sharp objects, better you than me*, he thinks. "That's amazing!" he says instead. "Where did you learn to do that?"

"Thanks," MacGregor says with a little bow. "Folk Dancing Through the Ages."

"I didn't know you took that class."

"You never asked."

"What else don't I know?"

MacGregor's mouth curves into a smirk. "A lot."

Awe flashes MacGregor a dirty look. "Ha ha. You know we better get out of here before Evangeline and the gang shows up."

"I really want to stick around and meet the Angel," MacGregor admits.

"Yeah, well, I would like that too, but we need to leave."

"Alright," he concedes with some disappointment. "So, do we play golf before we eat, or eat before we play golf?"

"Good question. Probably eat before we play golf."

"Good idea. Should we invite Harry?"

Awe looks shocked by the question. "Like duh! Harry would be totally offended if we excluded him. Golf is his passion."

"That and tennis and swimming and baseball and let us not forget, driving fast cars."

"True. The man is a sports dynamo."

MacGregor calls out to Harry to join them and a moment later he is standing on the sand with them. "Nice outfit," he says to MacGregor.

"Thanks."

"What's with fiery whatcha-ma-call-its in your hands?"

Awe proceeds to lavish praise about his fellow Guide's fire dancing.

"Sorry I missed it," Harry says with genuine interest in his Guide friend's activity.

"Actually," MacGregor says with a serious look on his face, "I'm thinking of doing a repeat performance later."

"Glad to hear it. You might want to switch to a night sky and darkness, so they can stand out better."

MacGregor practically gleams. "Great idea!"

"Happy to be of service. So, what's up?" Harry asks.

Awe decides to answer. "We are getting some food and then playing some rounds of golf. Thought you might want to join us."

Harry grins and proceeds to perform a happy dance. "Totally. You guys are the best!"

Before zipping off, the boys trade their current looks for old-fashioned golf attire, complete with argyle patterned vests and socks, caps, puffy knickers and oxford-looking shoes with spikes. If they weren't so incredibly handsome, they would all look ridiculous.

The stage is set. August arrives first, in full and stunning physical form versus his usual light body. He's wearing colorful beachy attire to promote relaxation and better blend into his tropical surroundings. The frozen fruity beverage he now holds in his hand completes the picture.

Evangeline shows up soon after, wearing a simple sundress with strappy sandals. She eyes August curiously and then takes a seat beside him. Neither says a word while they wait for their guests to arrive. Both of them decided to get there early. While August seems quite content with his choice, Evangeline is starting to lose patience.

August slurps at the last vestiges of his frosty beverage a little too loudly for Evangeline's comfort.

"Do you have to do that?" she asks.

"Do what?"

"Make that noise."

"I'm trying to get every drop," he says. "It's really good. You should try some."

"No thanks. Besides, you've had enough for everyone."

August gives her a dirty look. "Geez, I only had three. And it's not like there's calories or other stuff like that here. I don't see why I can't enjoy myself."

Evangeline just rolls her eyes.

"I saw that."

"Good."

Before their sarcastic banter could take on a more elevated crank factor, an exquisite female form appears before them. Glowing from head to toe, the dark haired, blue-eyed Angel smiles and then introduces herself as Serena. August and Evangeline are hit with an immediate and wonderful feeling of peace and calm. So overtaken with the gloriousness of what they are experiencing, neither can muster even a word for a few moments.

Finally, Evangeline recaptures her voice and clarity of thought and says, "Welcome Serena, thank you for helping us out here."

"It is my pleasure," the Angelic beauty says with an even brighter smile, all the while sending out another infusion of peace. "It's quite lovely here," she says joyfully as she swirls in place with arms outstretched and hands fluttering up and down in waves. Her wispy, multi-layered, aqua colored dress flows with her in a mesmerizing and soothing circle.

Evangeline explains that it belongs to some Guide friends of theirs, who thought it might serve their purposes well. She then tells Serena how they call it the Isle of Aaah, at which the Angel giggles and proclaims it to be perfect.

August offers the heavenly visitor a frozen beverage. Surprisingly, she decides to give one a try. Not knowing which one to give her, he hands her two of his favorites, one with strawberry and watermelon and another with pineapple and coconut. He cautions her to sip slowly and explains the concept of brain freeze.

After taking a taste of each, the field around Serena's body glows even brighter and her smile becomes wider. "Yum. Yum," she declares. "These are wonderful. I am not sure which one I like the best. Thank you, August."

"You are welcome. Would you like a s'more?"

"I've heard of those things. They're like sandwiches, only they are sweet and there's no bread, right? They contain some sort of cracker and chocolate, and something called marshmallow I believe. Perhaps I should try one."

"They are warm, gooey and amazing. Trust me. You will love s'mores," he proclaims before handing her one. "It's going to ooze, just go with it."

The Angel takes a bite and as expected, chocolate runs out of the corners of her mouth while crumbs and sticky charred marshmallow coat her ever-smiling lips. "Oh my," she gasps. "This is well, I don't think there's a word for it."

"It's the bomb!" he practically shouts, grinning ear to ear.

Serena looks at him strangely. Obviously, she is confused by his declaration. "I don't understand. This is not a destructive force. This is sheer bliss."

"Yeah, sorry about that. The bomb also means something really awesome."

"Oh, I see. Yes, this is the bomb."

Evangeline watches August and Serena go back and forth talking about food and beverages and wonders if she's gone mad. "Tom should be here shortly," she reminds them. "Did Melodia bring you up to date on the situation?"

Serena nods and then wipes her mouth before speaking. "Yes, she did. Poor Tom. Poor Helen. Poor Happy Juice drinkers. It's an awful situation."

"It is. Hopefully, we can put it to rest soon."

Tom arrives a few moments later. He scans all around him and soaks in the unusual and rather beautiful scenery of the place. A strange feeling of calm and peace fills every corner of his being. If he didn't know any better, he would think he just took a gulp of the Happy Juice he used to help create.

He stares curiously at the man and woman seated at the table as well as the apparent Angel who stands close beside them. Surprisingly, the Angel, who is grinning rather excitedly, is slurping some frozen tropical drink all the while licking at her fingers which seem to be covered in chocolate. Tom has no clue what is going on.

"Um, I'm here for the interview," he announces almost in a question as his facial expression shows his complete confusion.

"Yes, Tom, thank you for coming here," Evangeline finally says. "May I offer you something to drink or eat perhaps?"

Serena chimes in. "The s'mores are the bomb! That means they're awesome."

"Yes, I know," he says with a half smile of amusement. "I think I'll pass, thank you. Is there a reason why we are doing this on this island versus at a normal office type location?"

Evangeline once again speaks. "Offices are so, you know, officey. We thought it would be a nice change of scenery."

"I see. So, no offense, but what's with the Angel?"

Serena smiles. Then a lovely warm rush of peace and calm envelopes Tom's entire being. "No offense taken," she says. "I'm just helping Evangeline and August with their investigation. Lots of stress and emotions run high in these sorts of situations. It was thought that I could keep things calm and thus make this whole thing easier and more productive."

Tom seems satisfied with her explanation and decides to take a seat. "Ok, so ask me what you want to ask me."

Both August and Evangeline are impressed by Serena's explanation and relieved by Tom's response. With confidence under their belts so to speak, they decide to dive right in with the questions.

"Are you aware that the Distillery is currently closed for production?" August begins.

"Sure. I've heard a few things."

"Did you hear why?" Evangeline asks.

Tom shrugs. "Something about a bad batch of Happy Juice causing some bad reactions, oh and Contracts for Earthly incarnations have come to a halt."

"Very good. So, how does it make you feel?"

"How does what make me feel?"

"How do you feel about the fact that Contracts and Happy Juice production are on hold?"

"Honestly, I couldn't care less," Toms says a little too angrily.

Serena tries to send him some positive energy to prevent him from getting too upset.

August studies Tom's face and says, "you say, you don't care, but you seem kind of angry. Why is that?" Evangeline nearly panics by his question and gives August a look of caution.

"Happy Juice is a smoke screen," Toms states as simply as someone saying the sky on Earth is blue. "People should see clearly and know what they are getting into before jumping to that disgusting planet."

"Pretty strong words for someone who helped produce Happy Juice for at least ten years."

"Yeah well, things change. Souls learn."

"What have you learned Tom?" August asks.

"I can no longer be a party to creating something that tricks souls into agreeing to unimaginable suffering."

"What changed your mind?" Evangeline asks with some hesitation, knowing the answer already.

Tom starts to cry as he proceeds to tell them about Helen. "It's my fault," he declares with a shudder.

"It's not your fault Tom," Serena interjects all the while sending him peace, "It was her choice."

"A choice that was made far too easy by Happy Juice, but in reality, was not a choice at all. She never should have agreed to experience such horrors and I know she never would have, had she not drunk that stupid Happy Juice."

"Perhaps," August says with as much compassion as he can muster. "But you didn't make her drink it. There is nothing for you to be guilty about. I know it can be unbearable to see someone you love in such pain, but I also know our Infirmary is amazing and Helen will be alright eventually. You can't keep beating yourself up."

"It's hard not to," Tom admits.

"Tell us Tom," Evangeline asks, "did you get to a point in your anger and guilt where you needed to do something?"

"I quit my job," he says.

"Yes, we know. But did you do anything else?"

"What are you asking me?"

August looks nervously at Tom before asking. "Did you sabotage the Happy Juice?"

Tom's face registers total shock. "Are you crazy? Why would I do that?"

"To make a point," August offers. "To stop souls from venturing to Earth without a smoke screen, as you call it. To prevent others like Helen from experiencing overwhelming trauma."

Now Tom is angry. "Let me get this straight. I am already feeling guilty for contributing to Helen's suffering and I suddenly get a brilliant idea to cause more suffering. And oh, by the way, I do this because there is a greater good in stopping the use of Happy Juice in Contract negotiations for Earthly incarnations. Are you high on Happy Juice yourselves?"

Serena sends a wave of calm and peace to everyone at the table.

Tom glares at her. "Stop doing that!"

Serena's usual happy expression becomes crest fallen.

"I apologize, Serena," he says quickly. "But I need to be able to think clearly and speak freely without all that good stuff you keep sending my way."

Serena nods with understanding.

Evangeline decides to speak. "I understand why you are angry Tom. But you need to understand, we are just trying to get to the bottom of this. Despite your indignation, you must admit you had the motive, means and opportunity to pull off something like this."

"That may be so, Evangeline. But I didn't do it. And no matter how angry and despaired I have been, I never would have caused anyone else to suffer, even if it ultimately prevented others from suffering in the future. That's not who I am."

"Maybe so. But sometimes desperate times lead to desperate measures."

"I didn't do it," Tom says firmly. "Now, if you will excuse me, I need to get back to the Infirmary." He stands up. Then with a flash Tom disappears.

"That went well," August says with a look of defeat on his face, "not!"

GOOD NEWS AND BAD NEWS

"On a positive note," Evangeline tells her team, "everyone who was negatively impacted by the tainted Happy Juice is now totally recovered and back to normal. They are all resting comfortably in their respective Other Side homes as I speak."

Hearing such wonderful news, the team shouts in harmony, "Yay, O-bray-em!"

"Yes, well, he is good. Moving on now. In response to what we've uncovered, a few changes have already been implemented in an effort to avoid issues in the future. For example, the Happy Juice Distillery has put in place increased security measures. They will also be conducting tests prior to shipping out their product to Contracts to ensure they are not passing along something that's been tampered with."

She pauses briefly before continuing. "Moreover, all intermediary emotional garbage holding tanks on the Other Side have been secured and will now be emptied daily. Logging has also been enhanced and will be done automatically by system sensors when a change has been detected. All entries will be sent off to a secure location that is unknown to healing center and Infirmary employees."

"As for the main holding facility on plane 6," she says, "they have committed to doing more frequent purges of the potent emotional leftovers. In fact, I've been told they are now considering full cleanouts on a weekly basis. They will also be implementing increased security measures and improved logging processes."

Abe speaks up. "All of that sounds great, but are we any closer to figuring out who did this in the first place and why?"

August decides to answer. "Unfortunately, we cannot be certain about the 'who' at this point. We have our suspicions, but we cannot prove them yet. As to the 'why', given the 'how', we have a few ideas there as well. We are doing our best to narrow things down as quickly as we can. It's just going to take more time. At least knowing the 'how', we are able to employ protective measures so that things can go back to normal in the near future."

"I thought we had two really strong suspects," Bella wonders out loud. "When you say you can't prove it, does that mean you want someone to confess?"

Evangeline chimes in. "In an ideal scenario, it is best if someone confesses. However, that's unrealistic. Frustratingly, this was so well pulled off, there is no trail or proof we can go by to wrap this up. We did have two good candidates, however, one of them definitely doesn't fit as expected. The other has motive, means and opportunity, but vehemently denies ever doing it. There are still interviews that need to take place, so hopefully, they will prove to be fruitful and lead us to final resolution. Until then, we will all need to stay patient and keep doing what we're doing."

"Can any of us pitch in to help get through the remaining interviews?" Juan asks.

August flutters happily. "That would be super helpful! We still have a pretty long list to go through, since we added the healing facilities and Infirmary into the mix recently."

To August's delight, everyone volunteers to assist his team.

"I don't know if there is much to it, but I heard this rumor," Vigo confesses with some hesitation.

"What is it?" Evangeline asks. "I don't care how ridiculous it may sound. We need to look into every possibility no matter how farfetched it may seem."

"Well, there's a movement, if you will, that's been generating more interest as of late," he begins.

August interrupts his fellow team member from speaking. "Aside from the one having to do with Guides who just watch?"

"Yeah, besides that one. They call it the 'No More Earth Initiative' and make it seem like they have quite the following. Of course, that could simply be propaganda. It's not like thousands of souls have been seen marching and carrying signs about this yet. But it might be a concern."

"The leader of the group calls himself Blade. His perspective is that souls are done with the whole Earth thing and have been for a while. He calls Earth 'one big, smelly garbage heap that needs to be closed so everyone can be put out of their misery.' Blade and his followers believe it's their duty to take up the torch and help end the Earth experiment once and for all."

"Alright. I think it might be worth a look. August, please add this guy to your interview list along with any of his key associates."

"Sure thing."

"I was wondering," Bob says, "now that things are secure, are Contracts going to start up again?"

Evangeline indicates that she will be speaking with MacGregor and Awe after the meeting to see where they are at. "I'll let everyone know when something changes. Is there anything else anyone wishes to discuss or ask?"

The entire team shakes their head. With that, Evangeline ends the meeting, and everyone goes back to work. August happily preps all his new volunteers before they head over to the interview site, while Evangeline initiates a communication with Awe.

Awe's smiling face pops up on her display. "Evangeline! How are you? How did things go on the island?"

Evangeline forces a smile. "I'm fine, thanks. Things went … They went as good as they could go, I guess."

"I see. What can I do for you?"

"I was wondering if the Council for Contracts have made any decisions thus far regarding starting up again."

"As a matter of fact, I just received a memo on that very subject. Essentially, it says that due to recent developments, the Council will be implementing changes to the Contract process. Apparently, all negotiation protocols have been modified to include both Happy Juice and non-Happy Juice sessions. They believe by allowing both views, it will facilitate more balanced and realistic perspectives when a soul is deciding what they wish to do on Earth."

"Really? That's very flexible and evolved of them."

"It is. Times are changing. They think we need to change with them."

"Yes. So, do they have a target timeline to restart negotiations?"

"The Council is comforted by the fact that we know how this has occurred. They are also feeling more confident about the new security and controls that are and will continue to be put in place. However, while they are not making our start-up dependent upon a culprit being found, they are nonetheless cautious about starting up things too quickly. I imagine it won't be long though before

Contracts continues. But for now, they remain on hold."

"I appreciate the update and I would once again like to thank you for the use of your beautiful island. Just so you know, we are continuing with interviews and hopefully, something will come up that can help us bring this to an end very soon."

"If there is anything we can do to help, let us know."

"Thank you. I will. Take care Awe."

"You too Evangeline. Have a good day."

Charles still has a few things to do before he leaves the Infirmary for good, but he can't seem to get his mind to quiet and focus long enough. He should be doing rounds, but no matter how hard he tries, he just can't muster up the strength and courage to leave his office. His not-truly-physical heart is racing and aching while his breathing has become strained. If he were on the Earth, he might suspect he was having some panic attack or getting close to a heart attack. But he's not on Earth.

As if that's not bad enough, his seemingly uncontrollable and growing sadness and anger is fueling within him a desperate need to punch something and cry. His now fisted hands are trembling, as is most of his body.

I am such a mess, he thinks. Charles knows he needs to leave, but he seems frozen in place and unable to move.

He tries to connect to Debra from his communication device, but she is not answering. *Where is she,* he wonders. *Why isn't she answering?* He tries again and then again, and still, no answer. Fear is now escalating within him.

"You are being ridiculous," he tells himself out loud. "She's fine. She loves you. She's not leaving you." But no matter how much he tries to convince himself that everything is ok, Charles is finding it difficult to believe. Now curled into a ball on the floor, all he can do is sob.

"Charles, Charles," he hears his name faintly in the distance. He lifts his head and scans the room for some explanation.

"Oh honey," his dear sweet Debra says, as she wraps her arms around him and gently rocks him like a mother soothing a frightened child. "It's ok. It's ok."

"I thought, um, I thought you were gone and never coming back," he admits in a shaky voice.

"How can you think that? I will never leave you."

"You didn't answer when I called," he explains.

"I was in a meeting. I'm sorry. But I'm here now. What happened?"

"I just can't do anything. I can't..."

She strokes his hair gently with her hand and presses a soft kiss to his quivering cheek. "Let's take you home."

"I have rounds," he says as tears flow down his face.

"Someone else will do them today. You need to come home and rest."

"Alright."

Debra kisses his forehead. "Stay here for a minute. I'll let someone know you are leaving for the day."

"Ok."

Tom paces back and forth in the Infirmary's waiting room. He's been there for too many hours to count. With growing impatience, he decides to check with the receptionist again. "I don't understand why I can't see her," he says practically shouting. "I don't understand why I can't speak with her healing specialist. What is wrong with all of you?"

"Sir please," the receptionist urges, "I need you to calm down and speak in a quieter voice."

"Well I need to see someone and not just sit here waiting endlessly."

"I understand. I'm sorry this has been so difficult for you. I have put in a call to our healing staff. Someone should be with you shortly. Please sir, please take a seat. It shouldn't be much longer."

"Um well, thank you," Tom says before he reluctantly and quietly takes a seat.

Hunched over with head in hands now, Tom starts to cry. His poor Helen. He doesn't know what to do to make this ok. As tears streak down his face, he tries to force himself to be brave and positive. But it's so difficult. Every bad scenario is playing out in his head and he can't do anything to stop it.

In the midst of his despair and doom, he suddenly hears his name. He looks up to find a curly brown-haired, green-eyed man standing in front of him trying to get his attention.

"Hello Tom. I am so sorry to have kept you waiting," the male stranger says. "Things have been a little busy and demanding around here as of late. My name is Leo. It's so wonderful to finally meet you. I am Helen's lead healing specialist. Could you come to my office so we can discuss her progress?"

"Sure. There's progress?" Tom asks feeling for the first time in months, a genuine spec of hope moving back into his heart.

"Of course," Leo says enthusiastically with a smile. "There is quite a lot of it, actually. Helen is strong. And though her path has been difficult, she is going to be alright."

Tom smiles and wipes a few tears from his eyes, and then follows Leo to his office, eager to hear all the good news he has to share.

16

ANSWERS

August stands over Evangeline's desk dressed in full Star Wars Jedi attire, complete with a light saber holstered by his side.

"Is there a reason why you are dressed that way?" she asks, shaking her head and wondering why she is surrounded by so many crazies.

"Absolutely. After work today, Katia and I are commencing our Star Wars Movie Watching Extravaganza. I thought it fitting to dress the part."

Evangeline is clearly confused. "But that's later today. Why are you wearing it at work?"

August smiles widely. "I thought it would be fun. Not to mention, I figured we could use a little more of the 'Force' on our side."

She nods. "Perhaps. So, anything to report?"

"Yes," he says excitedly. "We checked out Blade and the 'No More Earth Initiative' he's heading up."

"And?"

"And he is right up there with Larry O. A nut ball for sure," August says, while making a repeating circular gesture with his finger close to his head to symbolize the word "crazy". "Blade's also a big whiner. Like he's the only one who ever had a bad day. Please. Anyway, in his interview he applauded the efforts of the 'Happy Juice Saboteur' and was really sorry he couldn't take credit for it. He also let it slip that he has a family member who happens to work at the Distillery, coincidentally."

This gets Evangeline's attention. "Really? Who is his family member?"

"Eleanor," he says watching Evangeline's reaction carefully.

"The woman who runs the Distillery?"

He nods and smiles. "That's her!"

Evangeline is really surprised. "The one who told us about Tom?"

"The very same gal. She was Blade's aunt in his last time on Earth and was also his mother in at least three of his past lives. Lots of history there. As you can imagine, they are really tight."

"Interesting."

"I thought so too."

"Are you bringing her in again?"

"I am indeed."

"Good. Let me know when you are done speaking with her."

"I will my leader," he says with a salute before he flashes back to his interview site.

Evangeline can't help but chuckle. *And so, the plot thickens*, she thinks to herself.

It's been days since Charles left the Infirmary. Although he has calmed down a bit since then, he still isn't ready to go back and finish things up. Debra has taken a long-term leave from the Science Archives to be there for him. She tries her best to keep his spirits up and just make him comfortable, but it's not easy.

His therapist came by the other day to try and help, but Charles was resistant to pretty much everything she suggested. He just seems resigned to feel bad.

Debra manifested up some things for Charles to hit or destroy, hoping it would give him a productive outlet for his anger. As for his tears, all she can do is let them fall and reassure him.

Today, Charles is particularly agitated and stressed. If Debra were honest, he also seems quite guilty for some reason. *Maybe it's his patients*, she thinks. After all, he never wants to fail them. Being that he can't be there for them, she assumes he might be feeling like he's letting them down. But something is nagging at her intuition that tells her there's something else going on. She is not eager to press him when he's in such a bad state. Debra hopes he will just tell her when he's ready.

"Can I get you something?" she asks.

"No, thank you."

"Is there something you want to do?"

"No."

"Alright. Is there something you want to talk about?"

"Not really."

His short responses are getting on her nerves. Boy oh boy does she need a break. "Ok. Do you mind if I go take a little swim in the lake?" she asks.

"I guess not."

"Do you want to come with me?"

"I don't think so."

"Ok. Um, I won't be too long."

Charles nods and then continues to stare out into the far distance.

Debra follows the garden path to some wooden steps that lead down to a strip of beach at the edge of a small lake on their property. She swaps out her slacks and shirt for a bathing suit and then makes her way into the water. The temperature is not too warm and not too cool. It's perfect. Once she's deep enough, she starts to swim. With every stroke and kick she makes she feels better and better.

Water is always a natural neutralizer of negativity and she really needs it now. Debra moves through the water like a woman on a mission. By the time she finishes covering every inch of the lake her whole being is humming with renewed strength, peace and hope.

Unfortunately, she was gone far too long for Charles' comfort. He is waving by the shore now, trying to get her attention. Once again, it appears he's gotten himself into a state of panic and doesn't seem to have a way of getting out of it.

Debra rushes to Charles' side, searching his face for some clue. He desperately reaches for her and just sobs. She holds him for a long time and he finally seems to calm.

But then Charles looks at Debra with the saddest of eyes and proclaims, "I've done something terrible!"

"What is it?" she asks.

He just stands there looking like a little boy who just got caught doing something he wasn't supposed to do.

"Whatever it is," Debra tells him, "you can tell me. It will be alright. Just tell me."

"It was me," he declares as his eyes lower in shame.

"I don't understand sweetheart. What did you do?"

"I sabotaged the Happy Juice. I used the debris we collect at the Infirmary from traumatized patients. I made those poor souls feel terror and rage and despair. I caused suffering."

Debra could barely wrap her mind around what she is hearing. Her sweet empathetic, ever-selfless love is telling her he caused someone pain. "I don't understand Charles."

"I couldn't take it anymore," he explains, in a quivering voice. "I was so tired of hearing about all the suffering and tragedies souls experience on Earth.

Witnessing day after day the horrific effects of returning from that terrible place was just too much to bear. The depression and anger I felt could no longer be pushed away. I felt desperate. Somehow, I thought it was not enough to put these broken people back together again. I needed to do more."

Charles fidgets and then takes a breath before continuing. "I needed to stop souls from going through this ordeal in the first place. I thought to myself, how wonderful would it be if everyone just forgot about going to Earth and just stayed here. Then they could simply live in peace, joy and comfort and never suffer again."

"Of course, as much as I wanted Earth to end, I realized that others might not agree. I thought if souls were still determined to return there, at the very least, I could do something to ensure that their view wouldn't be obscured. Their choices would no longer be made to look better than they really are. Their eyes would be wide open to the reality of what they are signing up for. And if they still wanted to go to Earth, they wouldn't be doing so wearing proverbial rose-colored glasses."

"Tainting the Happy Juice was the only way I could think of to change things and get everyone's attention. Unfortunately, I also hurt people to make my point. And I'm not sure I can ever forgive myself."

Debra embraces Charles and stares into his tear-filled eyes. "You my dearest love are not bad. The things you've done are forgivable. What you did, you did because you are good and loving, and cannot bear to see others suffer. Unfortunately, their suffering became your suffering, and it didn't allow you to think clearly or even find a way to be at peace."

"You never meant to do harm. You only wanted to stop the pain for yourself and everyone else. I just wish you would have confided in me about how bad things got before you acted. But it's going to be alright."

"How can you even look at me?" he asks.

"Because what I see is one of the most beautiful souls I've ever encountered. Someone I am truly proud to know and stand by every day. None of us are perfect, Charles. No one thinks and acts in the best way all the time. We all need to learn and practice at being better. Every one of us needs to give ourselves a break. You need to give yourself a break. You my love, have done far more good than bad in your existence."

"But despite your good intentions and the good you've done in the past," she says as she helps him up, "you still need to take ownership of your recent choices and face the consequences of them. You need to take responsibility for what you've done and give people the answers they deserve and need. They need the truth. Only then can everyone move forward, and you can move forward too."

"Alright, I will. Could you come with me?"

Debra hugs Charles and smiles. "Of course. I will be by your side every step of the way."

THE AFTERMATH

Much has happened since the Case of Unhappy Juice was solved.

After undergoing therapy and receiving a variety of advanced healing treatments administered personally by O-bray-em, Charles is now one happy soul again. Debra made her leave from the Science Archives permanent, so she could be with Charles on a full-time basis. Both of them are engaging in only lighthearted pursuits and are having a wonderful time.

In light of what happened with Charles, all Infirmary workers are now expected to attend monthly assessments and healing sessions. This is done to ensure that no one ever becomes too overwhelmed or despaired again. Everyone is also required to participate in one of many activities the healing complex now offers on a weekly basis to promote fun and frivolity in its employees. The Infirmary has also issued a mandate for workers to take annual vacations, as well as three-month long sabbaticals every five years whether they need one or not.

Speaking of the Infirmary, now fully recovered and quite at peace, Helen has recently left the facility and has reunited with her truest love. Tom, by the way, is over the moon with joy and making lots of fun plans for their future. Helen finds it all vastly amusing and is eager to indulge him and get a start on their new adventures.

Former Guides Joanne and Paulette have left the Guide business for good and joined forces to form a band and make music their mission. They call their ensemble, "Happy Without Juice" and are dedicated to performing the most uplifting music they can find.

August joins them every so often to fulfill his unrealized Earthly dream of being in a band. Aside from playing the guitar, he also fills in on the drums whenever their regular drummer Neal needs a break. And while his singing is not as good as Paulette and Joanne's, August does a surprisingly good backup.

The entire Problem-Solving team has committed to supporting and cheering their fellow co-worker on whenever he plays. The music is so life affirming and joyful, everyone feels like they've been healed and washed clean every time they go.

The band has generated a lot of interest as of late and is rapidly building a loyal fan base. As such, the Stage has offered to allocate a slot on their upcoming calendar for the group to play. Everyone is naturally excited and has been practicing every day to ensure that their performance will be the best it can be.

They are calling their concert "Happy Aid" in honor of the large benefit-type performances that occurred on Earth. But instead of raising money, the band is hoping to raise happiness. Given what they've been able to accomplish so far, no one has any doubt that they will do just that.

Aside from August's new musical activities, there is an even bigger and more newsworthy change that has occurred in his life. He and Katia have moved in together. August now makes weekly stops at Nostalgia to pick up treats for his lady and is known to say gaggy romantic stuff to her all the time.

Evangeline is overjoyed by it all. She loves making kissy noises and saying things like "I love you. No, I love you," whenever he's around. August just smiles and says "Thanks" in response. No grumpy humphs or sarcastic barbs or anything reminiscent of the old August. He's positively delightful. In fact, to everyone's relief, he even gave up the burp/fart thing.

As for MacGregor and Awe, they're now having regular beach parties with Luau type themes on their island to help Guides blow off steam and better keep up their morale. Even their therapy group leaders are joining in on the fun, 'cause therapists are people too.

Incidentally, after recently receiving his fire dance training, Harry has committed to performing alongside MacGregor during every Luau party. Awe, not being a big fan of fire or sharp objects, is content to simply watch and cheer his fellow Guides on.

All in all, Guides' spirits are high, and the new dual sessions (one with Happy Juice and one without) seem to be working out pretty well. On another positive note, sign sending and acknowledgement seems to be more successful than anyone can remember. In fact, MacGregor is feeling so hopeful he thinks it may be time for a big statement on his part.

Vicky has done much healing over the years and has reached a level of trust and faith that she's never been able to achieve before. As a result, she has been experiencing more victories and even miracles in her daily life. MacGregor is contemplating sending her a kilt-wearing bagpiper to show her how proud he is.

As for Elizabeth, Awe is thinking he should do something grand for her as well. After all, her belief in the unseen and the magic of the Universe has not wavered, nor has her desire to help people change and heal. As such, she has helped many along the way. She's also worked through a good deal of junk herself. *Yeah maybe*, he thinks.

Doc B finally returned to the Mind Matters Healing Institute and was surprised about all that he missed. He has decided to stick around a bit longer than usual. More significantly and to everyone's relief, he has committed to carrying a communication device, so that he can be reached no matter where his impulses take him.

As for Evangeline, aside from her utter delight with the Katia and August development, she has finally let go of her fears and made peace with Earth. She even contemplates going back there one day but is content to remain on the Other Side to continue her Problem-Solving work and live happily and lovingly with Ellery. Ellery, by the way, has finally come up with an idea that he thinks is revolutionary, but it's all hush hush at this point.

Little David, aka Amalia, had a major victory of his own. After too many fretful nights, he finally mustered up the courage to confront his father. As a result of their strong and tearful exchange, the little boy's dad decided to go into therapy and have his children attend counseling sessions as well.

Lots of healing has already taken place. In fact, Evangeline and Veronica cried buckets of happy tears just the other day after tuning into the Earth Channel to see how the family was progressing.

To their utter joy and relief, they witnessed a simple but beautiful moment when David and his father and sister were lovingly and happily snuggled together just reading a story. Unable to help himself, Ellery cued the old Earthly song "What a Wonderful World" to play in the background as the scene unfolded. Unsurprisingly, it only served to make the women cry harder. But then afterwards, he gave each of them a big hug and a chocolate malted milkshake to make it all better.

Speaking of the Earth Channel, to promote a more positive impression of Earth and the Earthly experience, they've added a "Good Stuff" filter option to all of its devices.

This new feature allows viewers to zoom in on only good things that are happening on the planet. Other Siders can choose to look at random samplings of positive occurrences or narrow their search to a specific category, such as cases of extreme kindness, compassion or courage. There is even an option for demonstrations of playfulness and utter joyfulness. Naturally, children are a frequent feature of the latter.

After all, youthful hearts and minds rejoice in the wonder that is all around them. They delight in discovery and learning and fearlessly challenge themselves to do more and be more. Victories are celebrated without hesitation. Of course, children also fall and may not always get their way. But after they cry and maybe yell about the terrible upset and unfairness of it all, their resilience and determination generally makes them get up and try again. Their tendency for short attention spans and lust for entertainments doesn't hurt either.

Play and laughter come naturally to children, as does creativity and open-mindedness. Young ones also have the ability to find joy in the simplest of things and believe in magic until they are told not to or when life struggles dull their faith.

Children hold the secret to having a worthwhile life. Adults could benefit greatly by studying them and striving to be more like them. Keeping one's childlike enthusiasm and spirit could make a huge positive difference in one's daily experience on Earth, regardless of their age.

And finally, with all the controversy about Earth and Happy Juice, God thought it was a good idea to send out a memo. So here it is:

My Dearest Children,

Although I do not connect with you often, know that you are always in my thoughts. You are loved beyond measure and beautiful just as you are. Please know that I bear the heavy burden of pain from all who suffer and rejoice as each soul fulfills their true potential and finds peace and joy.

I know this is a difficult time. Much change is upon us and there is more uncertainty than ever before. However discouraging it may seem, rest assured that all is well sweet ones. All is well.

I am of course aware that there has been a question hanging in the air for quite some time and the current situation has only served to bring focus to it once again. Let it be known that despite recent escalations of concern, Earth will continue.

Though faith can become shaken, the promise of hope can help us carry on. Please know there is always hope and if we feed it daily, it gets bigger and stronger and more capable of affecting change. While change doesn't happen as quickly as we would like, when it does occur it is a truly magnificent thing, and without a doubt worth the wait. I find that nothing is more awe-inspiring than to witness the unfolding, empowerment and transformation of a soul. I have already observed countless evolutions for eons and expect many more in the future.

You see, I have complete faith and trust that my treasured creations will march on bravely, boldly and beautifully, and ultimately become victorious. Every one of them has the infinite potential, if only they would believe it to be so.

Each soul carries a piece of me within them to remind them every day that they are not alone and that they are all part of one big family. It also helps them recognize their worth and remember that their gift of life is to be cherished. Sharing a part of me helps them also know that each of them is unconditionally loved and has the power to achieve anything they put their mind to.

We have been sending new energies to the planet and adjusting Earth's frequency and the frequency and DNA of its inhabitants for quite some time. Efforts to raise consciousness and awareness and impulse people to think differently and make different choices for themselves and others will continue. We will not give up until the totality of the planet has shifted.

Yes, there is much more work to be done. And although the recent unrest on the planet could easily make people believe otherwise, progress is being made and will continue to be made. We have already witnessed amazing improvements that have resulted from our efforts thus far. And while this transitional period may be ugly in many ways, it is creating a new foundation for something that will eventually be quite spectacular and beautiful.

Let us focus more on what has been accomplished and what is good, and less on what is yet to be done or discouraging. I know a better world is to come. And much like a new bud sprouting out of a seemingly dead branch in spring, souls will emerge from the current darkness in splendor.

In an effort to help things along, we have just implemented what many view to be a long overdue change to the system. After meeting with all counsels related to the incarnation of souls to planet Earth, I have decided to accept their warranted assessment that enough is enough. As such, souls who lack any desire to change and relish in obstruction, destruction or the suffering of others will no longer be allowed to go back to Earth henceforth. A new dimension has already been created to receive these individuals upon their passing, so they can no longer impede the progress that can be made without them.

That is not to say that all challenges and darkness will be lifted from the planet once these souls are gone. But as they leave, there will be more people open to change and light. As such, there will be greater opportunity for things to truly get better and stay better.

Humans will eventually come to know that suffering is unnecessary, and that learning can be gentle and experienced thru more joyful and comfortable means. One day, though it may seem elusive or impossible, we will create a Heaven on Earth. Then instead of feeling dread or fear about journeying there, all will rejoice in the opportunity to be in such a wonderful place. And they will proudly call it home and delight in being there forever more. And when that day comes, we will all celebrate together.

But until that happens, I will continue to hold a space, and ask that each and every one of you hold a space that in the not-so-distant future, all human beings will learn to:

- Take care of themselves without pain, illness, weakness or fatigue, forcing them to do so.

- Coexist in peace and harmony with one another, respectfully accepting their differences, while building upon and celebrating all the things they have in common.

- Show compassion and kindness for others without being guilted into it or having something bad happen to them or the people they care about.

- Take responsibility for their lives and happiness and recognize that making the same choice over and over will always result in the same outcome.

- Pursue happiness, comfort and relaxation each day and focus on all the good things in their lives.

- Leave the past behind, live in the present moment and expect good things to happen every day.

Until then my beautiful children, be brave, be strong, be joyful and never stop believing in magic and miracles!

Forever yours,

God

P.S. Because s'mores are the bomb and no one who eats a s'more is ever unhappy... Sorry Annabelle. I was thinking we should impulse everyone on Earth and beyond to indulge in one at least once a week. This could be the important unifying piece we've been searching for. Just a thought. ☺

ABOUT THE AUTHOR

For more than 20 years, certified hypnotherapist and author, Dawn Wheeler has harnessed and honed the tool of hypnosis to help her clients transform virtually every aspect of their lives. Her first book, "The Hypnosis I Know" delves into the workings and power of the mind and her own unique perspectives and approach regarding the use of hypnosis. Her second book, "The Secret Diary of Francis Lovell" combines Dawn's love of history and understanding of human behavior to tell a what-if-the-tales-are-true story about an important but elusive historical figure. Now in her third book, Dawn uses a fictional framework to explore spiritual and energetic concepts and give voice to some of the more difficult aspects of the human experience. Dawn currently resides in Michigan with her husband.

www.ingramcontent.com/pod-product-compliance
Lightning Source LLC
Chambersburg PA
CBHW060251100726
47907CB00003B/842